Facing fear of your own dreams coming true.
Longing to hold on to a beloved best friend.
Wishing to repair a life gone off the tracks.
A lifelong feeling that you never belong.
The secret life of a gorgeous black cat.

Functioning as signposts along the rich and often twisted road of Kari Kilgore's imagination, each story in this collection explores a different area of fantasy fiction.

Ranging from Appalachia to Atlanta, from love to loss, they all touch on emotions or experiences readers recognize.

The (mostly) women in Fantastic Shorts: Volume 1 may start out in familiar territory.

But in the hands of this talented storyteller, readers quickly learn to always expect the strange.

For childhood friends who always wanted me to make up stories for all-day summertime games.

Thank you for helping build the storytelling engine in my head.

FANTASTIC SHORTS

VOLUME 1

KARI KILGORE

SPIRAL PUBLISHING, LTD.

CONTENTS

Intentions

KARI KILGORE

AUTHOR OF LEGACY OF THE LAND AND TERMINALIA

For Angela

Chapter 1

Angela Garcia breathed in the rich cinnamon and ginger aroma of her third cup of coffee as she watched her wife sip from a huge mug of Earl Gray tea. Bright morning sunlight streamed through the wavy paneled glass of the breakfast nook windows, filtered by huge oak trees older than Angela and Julie put together.

She'd grown up in this neighborhood full of hundred-year-old houses, a precious bit of peace right on the edge of busy Atlanta, but Angela was still delighted to wake up here every single day. Giving up their expensive, modern down-town apartment to move back into her childhood home had changed their lives in more ways than she could count.

This cheerful bright yellow room, the sleek kitchen beside them, and the entire house basked in the love and attention the two of them had lavished on everything over the past six months. Their silky calico cat Lorrie purred her approval from her tiny window seat in the sun.

With Julie leading the way and Angela's enthusiastic participation, the outdated and gaudy late-Eighties décor had given way to calm earth tones, wood, and stone.

An open and airy home office for Angela's freelance publishing and design business had replaced her parents' overly formal dining room, and most of the time she was glad about that.

Right now, she would happily plan a torturous dinner party for ten than face the deceptively simple project she'd been putting off for the past few weeks.

Julie's long blond hair was wrangled into a thick braid, a good match for her sensible and appropriate dark green khaki pants and tan button-down shirt. She thrived on the social interaction and structure that had driven Angela crazy in the corporate publishing world she'd recently left behind.

Sweat pants, a comfortable t-shirt, and unruly hair twisted into a loose knot suited her better than any work dress code ever had.

Angela focused on the corkboard on the wall beside the kitchen door, one of the clever and effective tactics Julie used to keep such a big project on schedule. Instead of long check-lists of things to do, contractors to call, or notes about samples of paint, the white board in the middle had only three words surrounded by drawings of balloons and fireworks.

Finished: House Party!

Her parents had visited a week ago from their retirement home in Florida, beaming in approval at all the changes. Even during the big gathering with all their friends and family, Angela had been distressed about losing her excuse to procrastinate.

She wasn't fooling Julie any more right now than she had that night.

"Nope, not a thing on that board you can use as a distraction, sweetheart," Julie said, leaning over to kiss Angela on the cheek. "The only thing on your to-do list is your own website. You can't exactly publish a photo book with no way for people to buy it."

"I know, I know." Angela put her elbows on the square table, made of wood salvaged from remodeling, and rubbed her face. "Maybe I'll have a nice email asking about a consulting job waiting for me."

Julie snorted as she got to her feet. She picked up Angela's coffee cup and held out her hand. Angela groaned and let her pull her off of the cushioned bench.

Bagel, their gray-faced yellow pit bull, yawned and got up off of her matching dog-sized bench to see what all the excitement was about.

"Come on, missy," Julie said. "You drove me to work when I couldn't drive myself a long time ago. Gave me a reason to get out of bed a couple of times, too. Time for me to return the favor."

Angela let Julie pull out her red rolling office chair, then sat and smiled as Julie wiggled the mouse on the black wooden desk to wake up the screen of her Macintosh.

That was about as comfortable as Julie Ramsey ever got with computers running anything besides project management and architectural drafting software. Bagel settled into her pink couch-shaped bed at Angela's feet with a long sigh.

"See? Listen to our girl," Julie said, standing behind Angela's chair with her arms around her shoulders. "You can do this, Ange. You spend all of your time taking care of everyone else, making other people's dreams come true. You definitely did that for me. Your turn."

Julie leaned down and scratched Bagel's ears. She stood and crossed her arms, raising one eyebrow.

"No jobs for other people today," she said, grinning to soften the words. "If you must procrastinate, you're free to write a little fiction. I've been waiting years to read something new."

Chapter 2

THREE HOURS LATER, Angela scowled at the screen.

"I just can't come up with anything I like, Bagel." Her dog yawned and howled at the same time, nose in the air. "You're right, girl, I guess it gets the information across. I'm just afraid people will fall asleep before they figure out how to buy anything."

She clicked over to her list of plugins. This kind of sales website was so simple to set up that just about anyone could do it. Making it work well and look great took patience and a pack rat's collection of modifications.

Publishing her own photography deserved more than a dull page and rehashed design. Part of her nervous procrastination was wanting this site to look as special as she felt, and wanting to live up to Julie's excitement.

She flipped the scroll wheel, hoping something interesting would show up.

"There's a new one."

She couldn't remember where she'd found this plugin, but the name certainly caught her eye. *Intentions*. The logo was a multi-colored cloud, not clear enough to guess what it might do. She clicked the description.

Intentions brings all the flexibility and customization you've ever wanted to your website and your life, and even more than you've imagined. Our easy-to-configure plugin lets you design and implement anything you can dream up. Not even the sky is the limit!

Angela laughed under her breath. A bit grandiose for a free plugin. There wasn't even an option to upgrade to a paid version. It was compatible with her website software, so what could it hurt? By the time she finished a groaning stretch, *Intentions* was downloaded, installed, and activated.

An awesome photo gallery was what she needed, a way to showcase her pictures and let people order both the book and prints. Angela read through the instructions, finding a spherical layout she'd never seen before.

She uploaded her book cover and several of the photos and clicked Preview.

"What the…"

Instead of the floating thumbnails she'd expected, she saw several more book covers, each with its own sphere of images. None of them matched any design she'd ever seen or created. They did look fantastic though.

She clicked the About Me button and shook her head, reading about herself as a best-selling author of books she'd never written. At least the part about her being married to Julie was right.

Angela leaned closer to read the fine print under the Preview button.

Click to see where your Intentions will lead you.

She frowned and sat back. The instructions for the gallery hadn't mentioned anything besides displaying her own images. Her frown deepened to a scowl when she clicked on one of the thumbnails.

The cover was strange to her, but the title of the book wasn't. *Perfect Tense.* She crossed her arms, absently rubbing at the goosebumps covering them.

That was what she'd called her first and only novel, hand-written in a journal in college. She'd never even typed the title, much less any of the text.

Angela clicked the image, expecting it to go back to thumbnail size so she could see one of the other covers. An animated page turned, and the chills deepened from her flesh to her belly. This was her novel.

Well, not quite.

She read a few sentences under her breath. Even after so many years, she remembered the words in remarkable detail. This didn't quite match.

The prose flowed more smoothly, so much more vividly, better than she possibly could have written at such a young age. Almost as if her novel had been cleaned up a little and professionally edited.

Angela wasn't sure if she should be confused, afraid, or pissed off. She stood, the loud squeak of her chair making Bagel pop her head up.

"Sorry, Bagel girl, didn't mean to scare you."

She walked over to the recessed shelves built into the wall between the nearly floor to ceiling windows, running her fingers along the spines of the books.

Memories opened up in her mind, each book giving her an image, a scene, or simply a feeling, as vivid as if she'd read it yesterday instead of decades ago. This was one reason Julie was so great at building shelves. She'd had to learn how to help Angela wrangle her massive book collection.

On the fifth shelf down, just below her waist level, she came to a light brown journal. Neat hand lettering proclaimed this to be *Present Tense*, by Angie Garcia.

"I knew it was still here," she said under her breath.

Aware she was right on the edge of breaking Julie's procrastination rule, Angela flipped the journal open and started to read. It was the same story, exactly as she remembered, with no traces of revision or editing.

Her face felt a little hot at how clearly this original version showed the enthusiasm and inexperience of a college sophomore. She hated to admit it, even inside her own mind, but the mysterious new one was far better.

Angela couldn't imagine who would not only take the time to type the book, but get it edited and somehow sneak it into electronic format right under her nose.

She hit the Escape key, and the cover was back. She sat forward, staring at the screen.

"By Angela Garsey? Come on now!"

She and Julie had come up with Garsey when they couldn't agree on which name to use, not thinking it up until after their wedding. Both wanted to get their names changed but hadn't gotten around to doing it yet. Angela didn't think anyone else even knew about that. She pulled her phone out of her pocket.

"Julia Ramsey here."

"Hey Julie."

"Hey Ange! What a nice surprise!"

"Sorry to bother you, but something strange is going on here."

"You're not bothering me, not even a little bit. What's up?"

Angela stared out the window, trying to figure out how to say it. She didn't want to sound like she was accusing Julie, but no one else could possibly be doing this.

"Listen, have you...noticed anything strange about my computer lately?"

"Today was the first time I've touched your computer since we brought it in off the moving van," Julie said, and

Angela could hear her smile. "You know I'm not Mac compatible."

"So you haven't installed anything or downloaded anything?"

Julie sighed loud enough to come through the phone.

"The only thing I've installed is the power strip you plugged it into. What's going on?"

"I don't know, I might have a virus or something," Angela said, rubbing the bridge of her nose. "I'll figure it out, sweetie."

"I know you will. Want me to bring dinner?"

"Yeah, that'd be great. Surprise me."

Angela couldn't find any contact information for *Intentions* on the screen, nowhere to click for more information or questions. A web search didn't turn up anything more than her virus scan had.

She glanced through the list of plugins again, wondering who'd told her about this one. She couldn't remember ever hearing or saying the name out loud, and her memory was usually quite good. She switched to her email and typed *Intentions plugin* into the search bar.

She clicked on a message from Kate Crabtree, the instructor for one of her first web design classes. Angela's digital pack rat tendencies had paid off yet again. A quick thank you note for taking the class, followed by a bunch of tips, tricks, and modifications for the next level.

Intentions was in the middle of the list.

Something tickled the back of Angela's mind, something strange that had happened to Kate. She grunted. Kate had been perfectly nice and helpful during the class and for a few months afterward before dropping out of sight. No one knew what had happened to her until nearly a year ago.

She'd been caught in a hacking ring that had broken into

personal computers to steal passwords and account information. They'd gotten away with quite a haul, for a while.

Lorrie butted at Angela's leg and chirruped at her, ready for her late morning adoration. She leaned down and picked up the purring creature.

"You're right, Lorrie, maybe she can help. Sounds like she'd know how to do something like this, huh. Not sure why she would, but still."

Kate had dedicated a big chunk of class to how to secure computers, websites, and accounts. Such concern made her turn toward hacking even more puzzling.

Much to Angela's surprise, another search turned up a public phone number. A woman answered on the first ring.

"Hello?"

"Hi, this is Angela Garcia. I'm trying to reach Kate Crabtree?"

"You got me," Kate said, laughing. "How you doing, Angela?"

Angela raised her eyebrows, uneasy about that laughter. It sounded a bit manic.

"I'm good, Kate. Everything's going really well. How are you?"

"I'm a lot better than I was this time last year," she said with that unnerving laugh again. "Still building websites?"

"Sometimes, yeah. I'm getting ready to publish a photography book here in a couple of weeks, working on my website. That's what I'm calling about, actually."

Kate was silent. Angela was afraid she'd said something offensive. Before she could ask about that, Kate spoke. Her voice was flat and cold, and somehow threatening.

"Why are you calling, Angela? I can't do much of anything online without someone watching these days."

"No, nothing like that. I came across a plugin you recommended called *Intentions*. I was wondering if you remember where you found it." This time the silence was even longer, long enough that Angela wondered if the call had dropped. "Kate?"

"Yeah, I'm here. Don't mess with that plugin, not for anything. Understand me? It's bad news."

Angela shivered, wondering if she'd stumbled into one of the creepy stories she used to write that Julie loved so much. Maybe even *Present Tense.*

"Seems like a photo gallery to me."

"Sure, it seems like everything you ever needed. At first," Kate said, her voice rough. "Trust me on this one. I never should have sent the crazy thing out to you or anyone else. Cost me a few years of my life. I wasn't the only one on the inside paying the price for messing with *Intentions*, either. Some of them are still there. You don't want to get acquainted with them, do you?"

"Well, no," Angela said, anxious to get off the phone. That last bit sounded more menacing than helpful. "I'm sorry. I never should have called."

"Don't apologize. Good to hear from you. I'll keep an eye out for your book." Angela had opened her mouth to say goodbye when Kate spoke again. "Do me a favor and delete that thing, okay? Just get rid of it."

"Okay, Kate. Take care."

Angela moved the cursor to uninstall *Intentions* but didn't click. She shook her head and leaned back in her chair again, causing Lorrie to squawk before she resumed purring.

She wasn't sure if the conversation or the strange plugin creeped her out more, but her own book showing up in a new and improved form was too bizarre and mysterious to ignore.

"Well, kitty, I'm about to break one of the rules of horror and one of the rules of cat. Too curious to let this one go."

She scrolled back to the list of people in the To: field.

The eighth address was a good friend of hers and Julie's who'd been in that same class with Kate.

She was making more phone calls today than she usually did all week.

"Angela! I'm so glad to hear from you!"

"Hey, Paula. How's it going?"

"I'm great. How's the fabulous girl I hooked you up with?"

Angela grinned, much of her unease after talking to Kate fading away. Volunteering to test out Paula's dating website was indeed how she and Julie had met.

"Julie's awesome, but you already know that. I don't want to take up too much of your time, just a quick question. Ever used a plugin called *Intentions*?"

"Used it?" Paula's merry laughter, a sharp contrast from Kate's, made Angela smile. "I built this whole business on it. Best thing I ever set up for my site."

"Well, that's exactly what I was thinking of doing. Since you're way ahead of me in this game, do you have time in your demanding schedule for lunch this afternoon?"

"Demanding thanks to you two telling everyone you know," Paula said. "I'd love to. One o'clock work?"

"Sure. You name the place."

"Peanut's, just down the block from here?"

"You got it. See you there."

Chapter 3

By the time Angela walked into the hippy chic, thrift shop-decorated tapas bar, Paula was already set up at her favorite table beside the window, smiling and chatting away with customers and employees alike. She'd caught Angela's and everyone else's eye in class a few years ago exactly the same way.

She was cute enough, with short, curly black hair and a little pixie face and body only made more adorable now by her pregnancy.

Her attitude made her irresistible. Angela had never met anyone so relentlessly happy and positive when it was never, ever an act.

The stream of traffic through the restaurant lost its Paula-centered flow as soon as Angela sat down, shifting back to normal random motion. When they'd finished their first round of small plates and catch-up chat, Paula folded her hands on her belly.

"So, why am I lucky enough to be having lunch with you today?"

Only Paula could say something like that and sound

completely sincere. Only Paula was that sincere, a lovely anti-dote to Angela's paranoid mood.

"Partly because it's been about a hundred years. And because I wanted to ask you about that website thing."

"That's right, now I'm even more intrigued!" Paula said, leaning forward. "Are you going to use *Intentions* for your new book?"

"Maybe. I do need a great photo gallery. Kate Crabtree did her best to warn me not to ever touch it."

Paula grimaced, the expression strange upon her face.

"That makes sense, Ange, with what happened to her and a bunch of her friends. Answer one question for me first. Why are you publishing your book?"

Angela opened her mouth, and a few seconds later both of them giggled. No one had ever asked her that.

"I...well, I think the photos are good. And I've wanted to publish something of my own for a long time. Years, really."

Paula was nodding, but she raised one eyebrow the same way Julie had that morning.

"What do you want it to *do*, though? Don't think about it, just say it. Whatever comes to your mind is the right answer."

"I want people to feel as good looking at the photos as I did taking them," Angela said, her cheeks turning red. "And I want to make Julie as happy as she makes me. I know that sounds silly."

"Absolutely not! I started my site because I wanted people to be happy. That's all it was. I didn't even charge any fees for a couple of years, remember?"

"I do remember," Angela said. "We just about had to twist your arm to get you to."

"It was worth it, though. I've been able to do a lot of good no matter how you look at it. And I'm telling you, *Intentions* was the key to everything."

"Come on, a photo gallery?"

"Not at all, not for me," Paula said, drumming her fingers on the paisley-cloth covered table. "There are photos, sure, but not until you get past the first part. You've been too wrapped up in Mrs. Wonderful to visit the site for a while."

"But Kate..."

"Kate might have used it to make the hacking work for all we know. You get out what you put in. Do me a favor, Ange. Change something in the setup. Take something out, add something that doesn't seem quite right. See what happens. But don't publish anything until you're happy with it. That's critical."

Angela blinked, not sure how to respond to such a bizarre suggestion.

"The way I'm using it now is—"

"No," Paula said, holding up her hand. "I don't want to know. You need to figure out how it works for you, same as I did. All I'll say is what you want it to do makes a huge difference."

"You're not actually telling me I need to have good intentions, are you?"

Instead of the merry laughter Angela expected, Paula nodded.

"I know how it sounds, but you're going to have to trust me. Just promise me you'll make the changes and see what happens before you publish anything. You can tell me if it was good or bad if you want, but nothing else. Deal?"

This conversation was making about as much sense as the one she'd had with Kate, but at least it was pleasant instead of scary.

"Deal."

Chapter 4

Angela got home much later than she expected, not long before Julie would arrive. She didn't have much time to test anything. For some reason she felt like she needed to be alone. Bagel laid her head on Angela's leg, wagging her tail.

"Well, I'm never alone, silly girl," she said, letting Bagel kiss her hand.

Her photography book was first on the row of covers. Well, changing that wouldn't hurt a thing. That one was actually just about ready to be a physical reality, much as that thought scared her. She dragged it into the trash.

Angela gasped as the screen reorganized itself. All but two of the books with her name on them disappeared, and the covers weren't nearly as great. Those were textbooks rather than fiction: one about setting up photography websites, the other about designing and formatting photography books.

The only other things in her gallery were websites and books she'd designed for other people. After the third group, she finally saw new ones. Perfectly nice, well-built, and effective, and every single one for someone else. Her goosebumps were back full force.

"What on earth *is* this, Bagel?"

Julie had said many times before that morning that Angela spent too much time helping other people make their dreams come true, ignoring her own. She'd also mentioned her fiction for the first time in a long, long while.

One of their rare fights had been when Angela yelled at Julie to stop bugging her about writing, not long after she'd left that awful publishing company. Her full stomach churned at snapping at her wife for trying to encourage her once the burden of a mortgage was gone.

Julie was the only person in the world who'd read all the short stories as well as *Present Tense*, and she'd loved all of them.

Her eye was drawn to the author name on the first design book. The author line now said Garcia, not Garsey. Angela clicked the About Me button again with a trembling hand, reading about a version of herself somehow still in her corporate job prison, doing all her work for other people.

The personal information at the bottom mentioned her living in Atlanta, but no mention of Julie at all. Angela's stomach twisted inside her at the strange word after her name, one her mind didn't want to understand.

Angela Garcia, widow. She was covered with sweat despite the cool breeze coming through the open windows. Instead of sitting peacefully in her chest counting out time, her heart was shattered into a million agonizing pieces.

Angela watched the cursor twitching on the screen as she moved her hand, terrified she was going to accidentally click Publish instead of dragging her photo book out of the trash. She dropped it at the top of the list, closed her eyes, and counted to ten. She finally peeked with one eye.

All the vibrant covers were back, and she was Angela Garsey once again.

She let out her breath in a whoosh, her whole body giddy

and shaky. Whatever the awful thing headed her way had been, she'd fixed it. Angela jumped when Bagel let out a low, breathy woof, then trotted over to the front door, her tail nearly whacking into her ribs.

"Hey Bagel girl! Hey Ange!"

Angela nearly ran to the door herself, trembling all over. It hadn't happened. Thank the gods, it hadn't happened. She had no idea what that meant, but the words kept thundering through her mind. She squeezed Julie tight.

"Hang on, let me put some of this down first," Julie said. "You won't believe what was in the mail today!"

After a good long hug and a kiss, Angela felt a tiny bit better.

"Guess what guess what guess what?" Julie said, grinning and bouncing on the balls of her feet, something hidden behind her back.

"What?" Angela said, laughing.

"Come in the kitchen and I'll show you. Sit down and close your eyes."

Angela did just that, too happy with having Julie home to protest like she usually would have. Paper rustled for a few seconds, air moved past her face, and something thumped on the table. Julie's hands were warm on her shoulders.

"Look," Julie whispered.

Angela opened her eyes and felt her jaw drop. The color proofs for her book, more than a week before she'd expected them.

"I'm just so proud of you," Julie said, wiping away tears. "Just looking at the cover, these turned out even better than I thought they would."

"Go through them with me, sweetie."

Julie pulled a chair close, and Angela turned the bulky pages one at a time. Everything was better than she'd imagined, the colors vivid and the layout perfect.

"You know, there's something about these, Ange," Julie said, wiping still more tears from her cheeks. "No matter how rotten I feel, I can look at your pictures or read your stories and feel better. Every single time."

Angela turned to her, tears in her own eyes.

"I didn't know you felt that way," she said, touching Julie's cheek. "That you still felt rotten or loved these things so much."

"It's all good now, don't worry. Nothing at all like before. I still get down, but as long as I have this, and you, I'll be just fine. Seeing you do this for yourself, after everything you do for me and everyone else, that takes everything bad away. Ready to let the rest of the world see this gorgeous thing?"

Angela stared at her lover. She'd been telling Paula the truth about her reasons for publishing the book, sappy as it sounded to her own ears. Everything good she wanted to do was for Julie in one way or another. Now the best thing Angela could do for her wife was to give herself her own best efforts.

"I was just getting ready to publish the website when you walked in."

"Oh, I want to see it!" Julie said, standing up.

"Hold it, fair is fair. Wait here for a second. No peeking."

Julie rolled her eyes before she closed them.

"Hurry up then."

Angela looked the site over, wondering if she should at least skim one of the other books. She hadn't ever written another novel, but she'd had lots of ideas.

No, that couldn't be good. However this thing was supposed to work, trying to cheat herself or someone else was surely not the right approach. Kate Crabtree was the best bad example of that, and Paula's charmed life was an amazingly good example.

Angela wanted to write the novels for all the right

reasons, to have the pleasure of discovery with each new story the same way a reader would. The same way Julie would. She moved the pointer over to the Publish button.

"I want everybody who sees this to feel as good as Julie makes me feel," she whispered. "Julie most of all."

She clicked the button, and all the other covers disappeared. Her photography book and sphere of images looked even better on the site than the fantastic proofs did. Angela felt no sense of loss or regret about the books that weren't there yet. She only felt expansion, joy, the possibilities of life and love opening up all around her. She turned and held out her hand to Julie.

"It's live, sweetheart. Come see how you make all my dreams come true."

REFLECTIONS

KARI KILGORE

AUTHOR OF TERMINALIA AND INTENTIONS

For everyone who has hit the reset button on life

And ended up in a far better place.

REFLECTIONS

The air in the abandoned house felt as thick and heavy as the knots of gray cobwebs in every corner. Jessica still caught glimpses of her grandparents' lovely old home, almost buried under filth and decades of neglect. Meager as the light filtering through the hastily boarded up windows was, she wished she couldn't see quite so much.

The grand, curving staircase, her family's turn-of-the-last-century pride and joy, was littered with piles of crumbling white plaster and mounds of gummy dust. The dark hardwood floor she'd so hated polishing was invisible under a bleak landscape of moldy cheap carpeting.

Someone had painted over the beautiful oak woodwork, a sin Jessica's eyes wanted to flinch away from. Hand-crafted wainscoting, fitted with geometric precision to match each riser of the staircase, hid behind clumps and drips of thick white latex paint.

The sturdy sides and handrail had escaped an amateur's paintbrush, but a thick coat of mildew and deep green moss did the heartbreaking job. Delicate swirls and curling patterns of wood between the rail and the stairs sprouted furry tendrils almost like hair.

The floor creaked and groaned as she stepped forward, reaching toward the broken heart of this once beloved home. Her grandmother had loved spinning the tale of her own father supervising when they brought the carefully boxed grand piano on board their Atlantic crossing steamship. Several children, many grandchildren, and dozens of great-grandchildren listened awestruck at the number of men required to move the massive crate.

Those children may have later grown frustrated or even bored with endless lessons at the ivory and jet keys. But every one of them, Jessica included, respected and loved the shining black piano.

Salt from her unnoticed tears exploded across her mouth and tongue. Jessica wasn't sure if the clammy, musty air or the bittersweet flood of memories had her eyes watering more.

The piano had been shoved unceremoniously against the staircase, perhaps in an effort to evict it from such a place of honor in the ruined house. Jessica saw gouges in the nasty carpet underneath, all the way through to the oak boards beneath. The once polished body of the instrument was mottled and smudged.

The keys had collapsed somehow, black and white meeting at an ugly angle instead of lying flat and smooth. The white keys, now closer to dingy brown, were chipped and broken. Jessica doubted a single one of the strings in the closed body was even attached, much less in tune.

She drew her trembling hand back, curling it against her heart. A little girl's voice inside her head whispered that maybe if she didn't touch the piano, she could still wake up from this dreadful nightmare.

She wasn't here for a piano lesson anyway. Whatever

was missing in her life, faded away somehow since she last spent time in this much-beloved house, wouldn't be found by practicing long-rusty fingers and brain cells. The floorboards groaned softly, more like a giggle, when she stepped away.

The house laughing at her fear.

Or her courage.

Jessica turned in a slow circle, no longer bothering to fight her tears. The family room, with the wide fireplace that hosted so many of the family Christmas stockings bricked up. The front door, with the rows of sparkling rectangular glass windows full of corroded aluminum foil.

The graceful plaster archway that led to the formal dining room, full of oak and china and crystal in her memory. The room now empty of everything but filth and dust, the archway cracked in several places.

Staying down here, walking further into the glorious house of her memories that was now crumbing itself to pieces, wouldn't do anything but break Jessica's heart. Keep breaking it, truly.

The first fissure had torn through her chest when she saw the weedy, barren state of a yard that won neighborhood competitions every year when she was a girl. Every step she'd taken since had only crushed the pieces smaller and smaller, like these drifts of plaster all over the floor.

Nothing so ordinary or mundane as the constant nostalgia of turning forty had forced Jessica's feet up the curving stone walkway now covered with moss and mud. The unexpected call from a realtor, telling her the family house was finally for sale, had jolted her out of a routine life she didn't understand or care about any more.

She'd woken the next morning with this destination blazing inside her head – and heart – like the sun breaking through blackest October storm clouds.

Since then, only one movie had been running in her mind's eye.

Jessica had never understood what happened. Not almost thirty years ago, and not now. She never thought about her single dramatic adolescent fainting spell unless her brother or her parents laughed about it.

Once the memory was dragged out of storage deep down in her heart, the compulsion to come back here had taken over everything else in her mind.

Her heart-wrenching circle slowed, stopped. Jessica stood facing the curving staircase, her eyes searching for signs anyone else had been here in the last decade. A footprint in the thick dust, a depression in the blizzard of decay and destruction.

Not even the most delicate traces of spiders passing by marked the stairs. If any had ever inhabited the acres of cobwebs hung throughout the space, they'd long since drained the last drops of vitality and life away.

Jessica stepped toward the staircase, hearing the real estate agent's words over and over again. Foundation intact. Walls and staircases sturdy. True family heirloom.

The housing market crash had finally ended the nasty property dispute that left the house in such ruin. Great investment for the person willing to put in the hard work. The rare person who had managed to avoid the financial nightmare of the last few years and enter the 2010s with the means to take it on.

That had all sounded perfectly safe sitting in his office with bright lights, climate control, and tasteful fragrances wafted through the crackling dry air. And she *had* contacted him almost ten years ago, after all, long before she could have afforded such a great investment. She'd asked him to keep a watch on the house, even though she didn't know why at the time.

She still didn't know why.

She reached for the bannister, focusing at her bare left ring finger after telling herself for the last six months that she would stop. After all, she'd been the one to ask for the divorce, not Kyle.

Jessica had been right about that, too, and the one brave enough to say it. They both knew one year, five years, ten more years wasted trying to force their marriage to work wouldn't have made any difference. No matter how much both her parents and Kyle's wanted it to.

The fact that Kyle stopped calling long before she stopped staring at her hand surely justified Jessica's decision. She wished it felt that way, especially in the middle of the night.

Dull as that decade and plans of a future with him may have been, at least they were plans. Something to focus on and work toward. The drifting, endless boredom that settled in instead left Jessica feeling like her mind and everything around her was stuffed full of dull, clammy cotton balls.

Her fingertips touched the wood, sinking into the furry mold. Jessica gripped the rail, willing her hasty breakfast of toast and overly sweet hotel coffee to stay right where it was. Her heart pounded in her ears as she settled one foot onto the first broad, curving step.

Holding her breath and her right hand against the slick, sloppy latex paint obscuring the wainscoting, Jessica shifted her weight and stepped up. Her booted foot squeaked a little against the wood, but she heard no creaks or groans.

The staircase curved up into darkness, the gloom of the yard and the first floor concentrating into a vile black hole over her head. Jessica knew if she could make it to the second floor, the row of windows up there would light her way. Fifteen steps ahead still loomed like a reversed descent into hell.

The wall that matched the shape of the stairs held windows of its own that used to overlook a miniature orchard in the yard below. Cherries, apples, plums, even a couple of apricot trees. Now the sloppy changes that marred those sweet memories continued in cheap plywood boards nailed right into the window frames.

Jessica slipped her smartphone out of her jeans pocket, but she didn't activate the flashlight. Avoiding seeing the filth scraped away by each of her footsteps sounded more like a kindness than a risk. She held her hand up, thumb poised above the screen. More for keeping cobwebs out of her face than for lighting her way.

Jessica's childhood rose all around her. Every cautious step into the darkness sent her disappointing present falling away from her mind, heart, and body.

Colors brighter, sounds more harmonious, smells and tastes so much sweeter. All the choices and decisions of her life still ahead, all wide open and joyful with possibility.

Her rational adult mind longed to reject those memories as unrealistic. Nothing but wistful nostalgia. Typical symptoms of a recent divorce, turning forty, and needing to believe everything was better in days gone by.

The truth was Jessica's childhood had been pretty damn good. It was the grownup part she wasn't all that great at.

She jumped and nearly screamed when her fingertips brushed a rough, scratchy surface. Before her imagination could conjure a broad-shouldered monster blocking her way, she turned the phone's flashlight on.

Visual input only made things worse for a few seconds.

A solid blood-red wall rose in front of her, fuzzy and streaked with hair and mildew. Jessica remembered to get a solid grip on the handrail before she leaned back to get a better look. She finally recognized one of her cousin's old college blankets when she spotted the faded orange logo in the middle. She'd never liked the coarse wool, like sandpaper against her skin, even when she wasn't surprised by it.

Wondering why the silly thing was still here faded as soon as she managed to pull the blanket aside and step through. More bright yellow sunlight than she expected flooded the hallway with every door standing open. The gleaming hardwood floor reflected light halfway up the white plaster walls, and the long, flowery rug down the middle seemed to be in good shape, too.

The smell was even a thousand times better. She breathed in fresh air and faint lavender perfume instead of mold and rot.

Jessica thumbed her phone light back off and turned, half expecting to see the dingy staircase she'd just climbed transformed to its long-ago beauty. No, only an ancient burgundy wool blanket, moth-eaten around the edges.

She looked down, concentrating on her boots. Her adult-sized boots, the leather worn and comfortable with many miles under the soles. She saw bits of the dust and dirt she'd just walked through around the edges.

A few hesitant steps forward brought her even with the first door on the left, the dark six-paneled oak and brass knob shiny with care. Jessica's feet and legs felt like they were a mile away as she peeked inside.

The tiny guest room was as jammed full of furniture as when she was a girl, all clean and in perfect condition. The narrow iron bed with a knobby pink bedspread stood right next to a tall chest of drawers, with a compact desk and chair wedged against the wall. All the same, along with the sheer white curtains pulled back away from windows on two walls.

Jessica was surprised to see the same conditions and time of day as when she'd walked inside through those windows rather than a drastic fantasy change. A gap in the curtains showed partly cloudy, early October afternoon, deep blue sky. She stepped forward and pushed the curtains all the way back with a shaking hand.

The small orchard was still there. Instead of magically transformed to its remembered neat and tidy condition, the trees were still full of broken branches. The ground underneath still littered with drifts of rotting leaves and piles of rotting fruit.

Whatever this was only affected the second floor.

Jessica startled herself by laughing out loud. She wasn't sure what she'd gained by eliminating the question of how far her personal insanity bubble reached.

At least no one had answered her laugh.

Not yet.

She stepped back out into the hall, trying to look everywhere and listen to everything at once. The manky blanket was still there, the house still silent. Jessica continued on a few feet, then stopped. Afraid to breathe.

The walls on either side of her were no longer blank white plaster, the slight ripple of old-fashioned lath boards visible underneath. Beside her and stretching down the hall she now saw bunches of framed photos. They ranged from the size of her palm to a couple of feet across.

Families were more or less together, but new photos had been tucked in wherever there was space. Color mixed with black and white, cat-eye glasses and bouffant hair with free-falling locks and rounded frames.

Except the color wasn't quite right. And neither were the hair or the glasses.

Jessica stepped closer, blinking to make sure her contact lenses weren't dried out and blurring her vision.

She hadn't seen anyone wearing gigantic glasses like that in years. In decades. Everyone who wore them appeared to have tiny eyes, too, distorted by the thick, glass lenses.

And the color was there, but shifted far to red and orange

tones. The images weren't quite faded enough to hide either stick straight or obviously permed frizzy hair. Not to mention lapels wide enough to threaten liftoff on a windy day.

Not a single photo was newer than 1980.

Jessica shook her head, trying to clear the impossible images. She glanced at her phone, still clutched too tight in her aching hand. Instead of a heavy black plastic handset with a tangled spiral cord dangling off the end, she still held a sleek glass face showing someone else's photo of a beach and the current date and time.

"What the hell is going on here?" she whispered.

Afraid to break whatever spell she'd wandered into, but terrified her mother would yell up the stairs for her to get ready for grade school, Jessica retreated to the tattered burgundy blanket.

Sure enough, the images on the walls faded away.

Sure enough, when she twitched the itchy fabric aside, the thick, rotting mildew smell from downstairs assaulted her sinuses. She couldn't see down the stairs, but Jessica was certain she'd be back in her current place and time if she went back down.

She dropped the blanket, closing her eyes.

Her current place and time was hardly her favorite so far. Getting stuck back in the disco era might not be much better, but that didn't seem to be a real threat if she could still move that curtain.

Maybe whatever had happened all those years ago in this house was finally going to give her a second chance. She didn't want to spend the next decade wondering.

Jessica held her head high, squared her shoulders, and walked into her past.

She glanced into each of the bedrooms, seeing nothing that surprised her. Perfectly arranged furniture that had been old when she was young, all neat and freshly cleaned. A rounded oak dresser in her mother's old room, the surface covered with bunches of Avon bottles. Collected and admired more for their shape than used for their fragrance.

The camphor and eucalyptus scent of her grandmother's Noxzema face cream crowded into her nose, along with her grandfather's hair oil, when she passed by their bedroom.

The fourth door on the right, nearly at the end of the hall, had to be her destination on this bizarre stroll through her memories. Jessica had stayed in that room from the time she was old enough to sleep alone on these visits.

The bedroom itself wasn't much different than the others. Same antique and well-cared for furniture, thin white iron double bed covered with a girly quilt her grandmother had made. Jessica couldn't remember the name of the doll repeated over and over again on the panels, red bonnet and patchwork skirt fresh and unfaded.

The movie blazing in her mind when she woke that morning, a memory she hadn't thought of since she left the confusion and drama of a teenager behind, hadn't been in this bedroom. She'd slept countless nights in here, over holidays, throughout long dreamy summers, sometimes during the school year when her grandparents could drive her across town.

Up until a few minutes ago, the strangest event in Jessica's life had happened not in the bedroom, but in the attached bathroom. She wasn't surprised that her heart beat faster the closer she got, and her face flushed hot and sweaty.

The tiny white hexagonal tiles on the floor and halfway up the wall were spotless. The matching pedestal sink and toilet with its tank high up on the wall could have been right out of a catalog from a hundred years ago. Jessica wasn't concerned about any of those, or the heavy claw foot tub she'd so loved as a little girl.

Her attention was caught and held by the mirror.

Oval and small by modern standards, anchored to the wall by shiny metal clips on four sides, the mirror was as flawless and perfect as that day almost thirty years ago. Jessica stopped inside the doorway, far enough away so she couldn't see her reflection.

She wasn't ready for that yet.

On that long ago day, she hadn't been in her normal thousand different places and miles away inside her own mind. Not caught up in the usual eleven-year-old drama that she couldn't even remember now.

That morning her mother had shocked Jessica by telling her the house was going on the market because her grandparents had to move out.

She'd never spent another night here.

Her brown hair had been long then, caught in that in-between phase when she wanted to cut it but her parents still wanted her to look younger than she was. It had also been starting to curl and take on the unruliness she fought constantly.

Jessica stepped in front of the mirror, staring into her own green eyes. She touched her barely shoulder-length hair, cut full of layers to emphasize the curl and keep it somewhat under control.

Back then, she'd been trying to brush out hair forced into one massive layer, struggling with knots and tangles it seemed to tie all by itself. Same thing she'd done before and a thousand times since. She remembered her grandmother's wood-handled brush with metal pins that scratched her scalp if she wasn't careful.

That day, Jessica had stared at her face in the mirror, recognizing her little girl cheeks still soft and round. Marveling at the firmer jawline and nose, hinting at the woman she'd become.

She'd raised her arm to start the morning struggle with her rebellious hair and passed out cold.

Jessica gripped one side of the cool white porcelain sink, watching her booted feet against the tiles as she settled into a secure stance. Now that the memory was clear in her mind again, she knew she'd smacked her head on the tub on the way down.

Knocking herself out in an empty deserted house would be bad enough. Who could possibly find her in a spotlessly clean house that hadn't existed an hour ago?

She took a deep breath, looked up, and raised her arm over her head.

Trying not to laugh wasn't quite what she'd expected.

Jessica closed her eyes, hiding the odd vision of herself with one arm waving in the air. She waited until her shoulder muscles ached, then rested her forearm on top of her head for a few more minutes to make sure.

Nothing.

She sat down on the side of the tub, smiling at her own silliness when she should have been years past such things. The overly sweet rose smell of the oily pink bath beads her grandmother always kept on the shelf by the tub floated all around her.

What had she expected to happen?

Jessica rubbed her shoulder, tilting her head to the left, then the right. Well, what had happened that day? She sat forward with her elbows on her knees, rubbing her temples. The memory played through her mind, almost a frame at a time, each clearer than the last.

When she saw and felt her little-girl arm reach toward the mass of hair, a ripple of nausea twisted through her gut and up toward her throat.

She'd heard that could be a symptom of concussion, and she'd certainly hit her head hard enough. But that didn't quite feel right. Some part of her hadn't felt right since that day.

She glanced up at the mirror, her gaze drawn to the reflection doubling in the beveled edge.

This time the nausea hit hard enough to make her jaws ache.

"I didn't just pass out," she said, her voice airy and weak. "I *saw* something."

Jessica stood, gripping the sink again. The porcelain felt warmer on the side where her hand had rested before.

Instead of staring into her own eyes again, she examined the reflection of the wall behind her. Above the small tiles, a white towel rack interrupted the shiny pale blue paint. Nothing hung there, but she remembered carefully arranging her damp towels and washcloth when she finished a bath.

No room for a mirror there at all, then or now, but Jessica's mind searched for one.

She closed her eyes again, letting the frozen memory spool out second by second.

Even as an adult, she'd never liked mirrors set on walls opposite each other in a dressing room or elevator. The resulting doubled reflection stretching away into infinity always made her feel...

Faint. And nauseated.

She saw herself raising her smaller arm, the metal brush pins glinting. Movement outside of solid reality caught her gaze, spinning her protesting stomach into open revolt.

Her reflection doubled, tripled, then jumped to more than she could count. All the versions of herself twisted away in different directions, as if all the mirrors in the world lined up behind her, then shifted just a tiny bit off normal.

Jessica only realized she'd stopped breathing when her heart pounded in her ears.

She opened her eyes on her adult face, blotchy and red with sweat beading on her forehead and upper lip.

From that second until now, she'd felt like she was out of step with her own life. As if she were endlessly circling in a huge city full of one-way streets, able to see the building she needed but never able to find the way.

All those versions of herself twisting off in different directions.

Some frozen, staring back out at her. Some turning and walking away. Others falling backward, eyes rolled back, faces deathly pale. Green eyes turned up in smiles or laughter, or turning red and filled with tears.

Did all those girls, all those Jessicas, keep going on in their own normal lives?

Had she gotten herself on the wrong path somehow, all those years ago?

Jessica couldn't recall more than flashes, snapshots of that day. Her mother's wide eyes and frightened voice. Her father touching the back of her head, his forehead wrinkled.

The sway as someone carried her downstairs. Searing bright lights in a gray emergency room.

The first clear moment was waking up in her bedroom at home, with her brother laughing at the television in the living room. The knot on Jessica's head had still been tender when her head touched the pillow.

She rubbed the back of her head now, fingers finding only a slight raised area.

By the time she'd been awake enough to ask about the house, all anyone would say was there'd been money trouble. Her mother's red face and sharp voice had not invited further questions.

Jessica had visited her grandparents in an apartment after that. She'd only driven by the steadily deteriorating house a few times before she'd left for college and never returned.

But she was back here now.

A real estate agent's call out of the blue didn't begin to answer why Jessica stood in an immaculate bathroom from a 1979 time capsule while the downstairs rotted and festered in the second decade of the twenty-first century.

She rubbed her neck, fingers lingering under her jaw. Her pulse was back to normal after she'd foolishly forgotten to breathe. She turned back to the tub.

She'd gotten her first real growth spurt that same year she was eleven, shooting up to her current height of just over six feet. Her parents joked about hearing her bones creak in the night. Jessica remembered the constant aches in her legs and back.

If she sat on the edge of the tub again, sat up straight and tall, she could still see into the mirror.

She could hold her breath again and see what happened.

Much to her surprise, the idea sounded a lot less crazy than accepting anything about the last few days.

Jessica sat, gripping the flat edge of the tub this time. The porcelain was smooth and cold under her palms. She took in a few deep breaths before holding the last one.

She saw her whole face, watched as her skin turned red. Her heart beat heavy in her ears again, but Jessica waited.

Now her eyes turned red, and the air felt thick and sludgy against her skin. A wave of dizziness moved from her head down through her body.

Her reflection stayed the same.

Her lungs hitched and protested inside her chest.

Jessica's reflection doubled, then shifted back.

Her heartbeat left dark spots around her eyes, and the dizziness flared higher.

This time when her reflection doubled, the other woman blinked.

Jessica blinked back, then let out her breath in a rush.

Her heart pounded harder for several seconds, and she was afraid she'd overshot into passing out after all.

The other Jessica watched, her face pale and calm, a couple of inches to the side.

When Jessica's own face and breathing were back to normal, she got slowly to her feet.

The other followed her movement until they stood facing each other.

"How did you get here?" Jessica said. "Why?"

"I was looking for something. You, I guess."

The other's hair was pulled back and she wore a purple blouse instead of a winter coat. Otherwise she looked just the same.

"Are you in the same house?" Jessica said. "Is it falling apart where you are?"

"It's in perfect shape." The other shook her head. "Mom and her sister want me to move in, take care of the place. Help keep an eye on the college kids who live here."

Another dusty memory floated down from Jessica's mind, words and feelings settling in her heart and belly. Her aunt arguing with her mother behind closed doors around the time she turned seventeen. Her mother asking her about her college plans over and over again, until Jessica yelled out her top out-of-state choice. The farthest away, and the most expensive.

Her mother had seemed relieved, even happy. The arguments had stopped, and Jessica had gotten her first choice.

Another decision that had never felt quite right.

"What do you *want* to do?" Jessica said.

The other leaned forward, staring into her own eyes.

"Something else. Something different. I don't know how we're here or why, but I know something went wrong a long time ago. Right here."

Jessica nodded. "When we were eleven. When we saw each other and passed out."

"I didn't pass out. I saw all the others, all of us, and I jumped. I pushed, pulled, whatever it took. I felt everything shift, my whole life settled onto a different axis."

Both spoke at the same time.

"But nothing ever felt right."

Chills raced over Jessica's flesh and the hair on her arms stood on end.

"Whatever I did," the other said, "I think it set us on the wrong course. I didn't really remember until I came back here today. I've stared into this mirror a thousand times feeling like something was wrong, but this is the first time anyone ever stared back."

"Maybe because I'm finally here."

The other frowned, dropping her gaze.

"I'm sorry, Jessica. I truly am. I was young. I didn't think. I messed up your life and mine."

Heat flooded Jessica's chest when the other started to move away.

"No, wait! If you did it once, if *we* did, don't you think it might work again?"

"I don't think it works that way. Remember those old books, the ones where you got to decide what happened next?"

"The choose your own ending ones," Jessica said, smiling. "I used to wish those were real life."

"Maybe they are, or something like it. If you skipped around, they didn't make sense. I heard a theory once that every decision we make branches off another lifetime. We turn left instead of right. Open a door instead of closing it. Take a job or turn it down. Big choices, little choices. Every time, a version of us makes the opposite choice, or at least a different one."

Jessica shivered. "Is that what we saw in the mirror? All those lives?"

"Maybe. The thing is we don't know what the others have done. What decisions they've made. Even if we could manage to change places, go back to our original paths, we won't know what's going on."

"But it would be something different," Jessica said. "Isn't that what you wanted, what you said just a minute ago? I've been feeling like I was drowning in routine for years now. No matter how I try to change things, I get dragged right back in. The unknown sounds a hell of a lot better to me than more of the same."

Jessica watched herself, brow wrinkled just like her father's, eyes unfocused and far away.

"I have to tell you-"

"No, don't tell me anything!" Jessica laughed, the first time in longer than she remembered that true joy bubbled up from her heart. "That day you didn't know what was going to happen. You just jumped."

The other smiled and laughed under her breath.

"And if we can manage this thing, what if everything gets worse? What if we hate our lives even more?"

Jessica sighed, all at once more weary than amused or even surprised.

"That would be feeling *something*, wouldn't it? Maybe if we feel something, we can change for the better. I'm willing to risk it."

The other closed her eyes for several seconds, long enough that Jessica was afraid she would leave after all. She opened her eyes and leaned forward again, nose almost against the glass.

"Me too."

Jessica opened her mouth to ask how, what to do, but she

leaned forward instead. Unconscious or not, some part of her had managed to do this before.

She already knew how.

The two reflections moved closer and closer until they merged, only the different hairstyles to tell them apart. Then they faded into a blur Jessica couldn't see anymore.

She focused all of her mind, her will, on wanting. Needing. On the restless desire for change that hadn't left her since she'd last stood on this spot.

All her teenaged anxiety, her adult apathy, pulled forward and pushed toward the mirror, the impossible reflection of another self.

Another reality.

Another life.

Jessica shifted forward until her nose should have met cool resistance.

Then she was falling.

She fell through thirty years and a single instant, into nothing and through everything.

* * *

Jessica scowled, certain she saw an odd smudge on the mirror. Inside the mirror, really, maybe a flaw in the antique silver backing.

She moved back a few inches and it was gone.

The antique glass really was in remarkable shape for as old as it was, just like the rest of the house. Her mother and aunt had done a fine job keeping up the place for so many years. Especially considering the numbers of college kids who had passed through, paying their share of room and board by helping keep the place up.

She looked around again, deciding she wouldn't stay in her old room after all. Her grandparent's room was much nicer. Maybe she was finally grownup enough to decide for herself where she'd sleep in this house.

She tucked a few loose strands of hair back into place, thinking she might try getting her hair cut shorter next time. She straightened her purple blouse.

As she turned to leave, Jessica caught her reflection in the mirror one more time.

For some reason she couldn't quite catch hold of, joy bubbled up from her heart.

Jessica grinned at herself, then walked out the door.

The Seeds of Love

KARI KILGORE

Author of Songs in the Mountain and The Dream Thief

*For Gosamer, Bella, Juni Moon, Bonzo, Golly,
Calvin, Pete, Buck, and all the other best friends to come.
And to go.*

Chapter 1

Virginia Evans sat cross-legged on the cold white-tiled floor, trying to ignore the ache in her heart and her backside. Her sweet dog Maggie, an unknown mix with a blocky head, floppy ears, and shaggy red hair that nearly matched Virginia's, lay curled up on her thick, green corduroy dog bed that went everywhere with her now. Despite the permanent coating of hair and doggie smell that defied washing, Virginia wished she could share the orthopedic padding.

And she didn't dare nudge her girl. She shifted to a less floor-bruised spot and stared into Maggie's cloudy brown eyes, hoping for a miracle she knew wouldn't be coming.

Even with the door closed, she heard the familiar din of human, canine, and feline conversation from the treatment area at the end of the hall. Virginia's family had been bringing pets to this veterinary hospital longer than she'd been alive. Her own history with Maggie stretched back seventeen years to when Virginia was a shy teenager trying to contain a wriggly puppy, one who outgrew her lap way too soon.

The diagnostic tools and equipment had changed faster

than she could keep up with over the years, especially with so many innovations coming from off-world technology. Still, the pale blue walls, angular black chairs, and huge selection of pet toys out front were exactly the same.

Maggie had gone through more than her fair share of the squeaky stuffed animals. She'd finally started keeping keeping her favorites over the last few years rather than shredding them to fuzz in a matter of minutes.

"You silly old girl," Virginia said, leaning down and touching Maggie's broad forehead with her own. "I wish I could put you in my heart and keep you forever." She jumped when a woman spoke behind her.

"Ms. Evans, I'm Doctor Rosa Martinez. Didn't mean to sneak up on you like that. I've got Maggie's test results." Virginia got to her feet with as much dignity as she could manage.

"That was faster than last time we were here," Virginia said. "Barely ten minutes."

The vet touched the wall over the gray-faced dog, and columns of abbreviations and numbers drifted into focus. Maggie's tail thumped when Dr. Martinez reached down to stroke her head.

"Good girl, Maggie. We just upgraded our quantum networks a few weeks ago, so everything's running faster." She tapped a section in the middle, and several numbers with greater-than signs beside them filled the space. Virginia and Maggie's usual vet been watching those numbers fluctuate for almost a year now. "I'm truly sorry, Ms. Evans. I wish I could give you better news."

"Call me Virginia, please."

She blinked, hoping the tears wouldn't start before she even heard the words.

"Of course, Virginia. You're right about Maggie having

trouble with her kidneys again. I'm afraid we're running out of treatment options for your girl."

The numbers blurred, and Virginia compressed her lips. She'd been expecting this for a few weeks now, and she'd foolishly thought she'd prepared herself. Her head and throat felt like they were filling with hot, heavy water.

"How…" Virginia stopped when her voice broke and took a deep breath. "How long?"

"You know her better than anyone else," the doctor said. "So you'll know when she really starts to decline. But I think we're looking at days rather than weeks."

"Oh, my girlie," Virginia whispered, dropping to one knee and scratching under the dog's chin. Maggie licked her hand and thumped her tail again. "Are you sure there's nothing else we can do for her?"

Dr. Martinez touched the wall a few more times, and a portal for the nearby vet school replaced the chart. Virginia's eyes widened at the estimated prices, clear enough even through her tears.

The vet shrugged. "Even if we put aside cost, which is considerable, Maggie's past the age range for most of these. Her heart and lungs likely wouldn't withstand the stress. I know this is awful for you, but it's a question of how you want her last days to be."

"I don't want her to suffer just so I won't." Virginia held her lips against Maggie's cheek for a few seconds before looking up. "What can I do to make sure she's comfortable?"

"What you're doing right now is the most important thing." The doctor knelt beside Virginia and scratched the dog's ears, smiling when she turned her head to one side, then the other. "She's in really good shape, Virginia, and she's happy. She's just winding down. How long have you had Maggie?"

"Seventeen years. Since she was a baby." She wiped at her

face and laughed. "Since I was a baby, too. I was only fifteen when I got her."

"Well, you two grew up together," the doctor said. "No wonder she's so happy. I'm going to send some information home with you. I'd be glad to answer any questions, but our counselor helps families through this process all the time."

Both women got to their feet, and Dr. Martinez handed Virginia a tissue.

"Thank you, Doctor. This is one of the bad parts of off-world tech helping everyone live longer. We'll probably make it to well over one hundred, but our pets still leave us way too soon."

The vet raised her eyebrows and took Virginia's hand in both of hers.

"Be sure to speak to Counselor Indurane before you leave. This is never an easy thing, but he can help more with your choices than you might think. You two can stay in here for a bit if you need to."

Dr. Martinez closed the door, and Virginia sat down beside Maggie again. More memories than she could possibly count, more than half her life, flowed through her mind faster than her tears fell.

High school, best friends, girlfriends, boyfriends, college, moving out on her own, getting married. Everything that mattered since she'd started working out her own life included Maggie.

"Don't know how I'm going to get through this, Mags. I wish Gowri were home."

The thought of her wife visiting family on the other side of the planet for another week was more than Virginia could take. She buried her face against Maggie's soft red fur, her matching curls falling forward like a shroud, and sobbed.

Chapter 2

THE COUNSELOR'S office door stood open, and Virginia felt a bit guilty about peeking in before he noticed her. The space was small and neat, with only a few books and folders on the dark wooden desk and shelves. The walls brought all the color and light into the space. Nearly every inch was covered with photos of dogs, cats, even a few rodents and reptiles.

The man himself had dusky skin, nothing like the rich browns of Gowri and her family. She wondered if Mr. Indurane's warm grayish complexion was entirely human.

"Excuse me, Mr. Indurane?"

The counselor smiled when he looked up from his vidscreen. He walked around to shake her hand, standing barely as high as her shoulder.

"Ms. Evans?" he said. "I was hoping you'd stop by. And this must be Maggie."

He leaned down, and Maggie licked his face with more energy than she'd shown in several days. Virginia puzzled over his accent. His words sounded precise, like a European fairly new to English, but softer.

"Sorry about that," Virginia said, smiling. "She's not usually that enthusiastic with new people."

The counselor laughed and kissed Maggie's nose.

"Nonsense," he said. "Sweet kisses bring nothing but joy to my life. I regret that we meet under such circumstances, but I hope I can ease the pain for both of you. Please, have a seat."

As soon as Virginia put the dog bed on the floor, Maggie circled her normal three times and settled down with a groan.

"First of all," Mr. Indurane said. "I'm so very sorry Maggie is coming to this stage of her life. I can plainly see how much love the two of you share."

Virginia looked down at Maggie's head, chin resting on her shoe, and hot tears welled up again.

"Thank you, Mr. Indurane. She's been with me for seventeen years."

"Dr. Martinez tells me you grew up together," he said. "This makes a rare and lovely bond."

"I've been lucky to have her with me this long." Virginia's voice shook, and she was desperate to change the subject. "I'm sorry if this is rude, but where are you from?"

"You're not the slightest bit rude," he said. "I came here from London, and before that from a planet called Braxia." He pronounced it with a rolled r and shirring sound. Bracksha. Before she could ask if that was one of the more distant seed-worlds, the counselor handed her a stack of brochures. "With apologies to you, Maggie. Nothing must be decided today, Ms. Evans, but these are some of the options we can discuss when you're ready."

Virginia squeezed tears from her eyes and took the brochures. She expected the usual burial, cremation, and tombstone packages. The information about cloning surprised her. She pulled those two out and dropped them on the desk.

"I'm not sure what we're going to do when the time comes," she said. "But I know we won't be cloning Maggie. Nothing about her would be the same."

Mr. Indurane nodded. "I understand. Many people have been disappointed with cloning in the past, and that continues even as techniques improve and cost drops. Such a commonplace procedure rarely brings the comfort they expect, at least not with their beloved animals. New options have recently become available, some experimental, that may be more appealing. I don't have printed materials yet, but I would be pleased to explain them to you."

Maggie raised up on her front legs and pushed her nose under Virginia's hand, her life-long request for attention. That was enough.

She couldn't sit here with her living, breathing girlhood best friend and make plans for her death. Virginia didn't even want to imagine that nightmare day, much less create some kind of script for everyone to follow.

"You've been very kind, Mr. Indurane, but I can't do this. Not right now. I'll take a look at these later. Maybe when she's asleep. I'm sorry, I can't."

He was around the desk and holding out a hand before she saw him move.

"No, please don't apologize," he said. "It is I who should be sorry." He took her left hand and she was glad of the support as she stood. "I've no wish to be forward, but I see your lovely rings. You're most welcome to bring your spouse to speak with me together if that would help you through this transition."

"She's out of town," Virginia said, the tears threatening yet again. She glanced at her pale hand in Mr. Indurane's, seeing swirling intricate henna on her wedding day. "She won't be back for a week. I hope that's not too late."

"I hope so as well, Ms. Evans." He squatted beside Maggie, and she nearly hit her ribs with her tail as she kissed every part of his face she could reach. "It has been a pleasure to meet you, Maggie. I hope to see both of you again."

Chapter 3

Virginia fell back onto the low, dark red couch with a deep sigh. Barely eleven on a Saturday morning, and she was exhausted. The living room in their small house wasn't much different from Mr. Indurane's office, with black metal shelves decorated more with photographs and books than anything else. So many of those photographs featured the black muzzle of Maggie's youth, gradually fading to the white taking over her whole face.

As if responding to a warning from her younger self, Maggie rested her damp chin on Virginia's knee. She drank more and more water and seemed to care less about being graceful about it. Virginia patted the cushion beside her.

"Come on, goofy. Dad's rules about no dogs on the couch at his house are a long way behind us now."

Maggie backed up, then walked carefully up three steps made of cushions that matched the couch. Virginia smiled at the memory of Gowri suggesting the makeshift staircase when they got the new furniture a couple of years ago. Maggie turned her usual three times before she settled with a deep sigh of her own.

For the first time since she'd first met her wife-to-be, Virginia dreaded talking to Gowri. Sub-light connections hid the extraordinary distance, but Virginia hoped leaving the video off would conceal a least a little of her upset. The last thing she wanted was to waste time trying to hide her puffy, red eyes before calling her in-laws.

Gowri's youngest brother answered on the third ring.

"Virginia, wonderful to speak to you!" Pravul said. "We all miss you here. How's Maggie?"

"She's hanging in there, thank you. Sorry to call so late. I miss you too, Pravul. Is Gowri close by?"

"She's out with Mother and our aunties," he said, his smile plain in his voice. "Showing our little sister a good time before she's off to the colonies. Might be a while. I'd imagine she wishes you were with her right now."

Virginia laughed, pushing her fingertips into the ache between her eyes.

"I feel exactly the same," she said. "Please tell Suni I love her and wish her good journey. I won't keep you. Can you ask Gowri to call me when she gets back in? The time doesn't matter."

"I certainly will," he said. "Take care, my sister."

"You too, my brother."

Virginia put the phone down and scrubbed both hands along Maggie's back. The corners of her mouth drew back in the canine grin that always made Gowri laugh.

She claimed that was how Virginia won her heart six years ago. Who wouldn't want the girl who made sure her dog was always smiling?

"I think she fell for you before me, Maggie girl. She's very smart."

She didn't dare say the next part out loud, too afraid the words would bring it into reality.

Please wait until Gowri gets home. For your sake, for hers. And for mine.

Maggie twisted and grunted until she was on her back. She stretched and relaxed all four legs, heaved a great groan, and closed her eyes.

"I hear you. Have a good dreamtime, Mags."

Virginia could just reach her backpack without disturbing Maggie. She pulled the brochures out, then settled back with one hand on her dog's white belly. Most of the choices were depressingly similar to what her parents had gone through with her great-grandparents. Burial or cremation. Casket or urn. Plaque or tombstone.

She felt the same as while watching the expenses mount for humans. The most important part, the soul, the personality, whatever people called life force, was long gone by that point. Spending hundreds or thousands on an animal felt just as silly as on a person.

The only appealing possibility was a memorial plant engineered with the genetic code of the deceased. She put the brochure aside to talk to Gowri about, and a list of company names on the back caught her eye.

The third from the bottom was *Love Eternal*, followed by *Coming Soon!* That must be one Mr. Indurane meant to explain to her. She felt a little guilty for running out of there so fast, but Maggie's warm belly reminded her why. Maggie twitched, all four white feet flexing in turn.

"I hope you're young in your dreams, sweet girl," she whispered.

The phone lit up, and Virginia grabbed the handset before it rang. Her heart pounded with hope that Gowri would be on the other end. She saw her father's face instead. She activated the video, not wanting to hide her sadness anymore.

"Hi hon," he said. "How's it going?"

"Hey, Dad. I'm okay. Kind of a rough day around here."

"I saw it in your eyes but was afraid to ask." He frowned. "Bad news at the vet?"

Virginia seemed to have a never-ending supply of tears.

"Yeah, just what I was afraid of. Not much we can do but wait."

"I'm so sorry, Gin," he said. "I keep hoping they'll catch up with longer lives for our pets like they keep doing with us. Is there anything new they can try? We get so many breakthroughs from off-planet."

"Maybe if she were a lot younger," Virginia said, taking a deep breath. "Or if we were a lot wealthier. Like you said, they haven't exactly focused on dogs. Hope they do someday."

"Well, she's certainly had a wonderful life thanks to you," he said. "When does Gowri get back?"

"Not for another week. That might... It's going to be close."

"What can I do to help, Sweetheart?" he said. "Maggie's as much my baby as you are, you know."

Maggie barked in her sleep, a soft, ghostly sound Virginia had always loved. Her father's question loomed large in her mind, combining with Mr. Indurane's mention of experimental options.

"Best sister I could have had," she said. "I can think of one thing. If you have some free time over the next couple of days, I need to make a few phone calls, take care of the arrangements. Want to stay here with the old girl for a few hours?"

"Of course, I'd love to," he said. "That gives me a chance to spoil her as much as I want. I'm free in a couple of hours if that's not too soon."

"That would be fantastic, Dad. She's holding her own,

but she needs a lot of water, and she goes out a lot more often."

"Just like when she was a baby," her father said. "We'll do just fine. See you around two."

Maggie nose and lips quivered as she growled in her sleep. Virginia smiled, wondering as always what had her so agitated. Her smile faded as she noticed how worn her dog's teeth were, how sharp her ribs were. The bouncy puppy, energetic adult, and even calm, sweet senior dog were far in the past.

The reality of life without her best friend was closer than she wanted to admit, even to herself.

Chapter 4

Virginia gripped the chilly steering wheel, staring at the sign for the school of veterinary medicine and research in the distance. The windows were fogging up, and she was getting cold. She still couldn't move.

She'd done everything she could. Asking more talented and busy people to review Maggie's records wasn't going to help. Even if she did have all the money in the world, Virginia wouldn't put her through so much discomfort. Starting the car and driving away would make everything final.

She jerked when the phone rang through the car's speakers. She recognized the number for her brother-in-law's house.

"Hey gorgeous!" Gowri said. "Sorry it took so long to call you back. These crazy women kept me out half the night."

"You have no idea how glad I am to hear your voice, Sweetie."

"Yours don't sound so good," Gowri said. "Has something happened to our girl?"

"Yeah, just what we thought last week," Virginia said.

Her voice was almost steady. "The medication isn't working anymore. Her time is running out, Gowri."

"I'm so sorry I came on this trip, Gin. I hate you going through this alone."

Virginia winced. The last thing she wanted was to make anyone else feel bad, least of all the person she loved most.

"You couldn't have missed your sister heading out for five years," she said. "I wish I could be there to see her off. I miss you, but this might make sense. Maggie helped me through a lot of rotten times when I was a kid. I'll see her through at the end. Anyway, she might hold on 'til you get back."

"Don't let her suffer for me, okay?" Gowri said, her own voice trembling. "I can't imagine our home without her, but you'll know what to do when the time comes. You always do. I want to see her again, but she knows I adore her. I gave her about a hundred hugs and kisses before I left, just like I did you."

Virginia smiled, feeling warm joy in her chest instead of hot sorrow for the first time all day.

"I'm going with you next time, Gowri. This is too long to be apart. Go get some sleep. There's no telling what you'll be up to tomorrow. Love you."

"Love you, Gin. Give our girl my love too."

Virginia took a deep breath, then started the car. Sitting there freezing to death wasn't going to help anyone. The only thing she could possibly do now, besides going home and cuddling up with Maggie, was find out if there actually were even more experimental options.

Only one person, or mostly person, could help her with that.

Chapter 5

Mr. Indurane beamed when Virginia knocked on his open door, his dark blue eyes sparkling. He took her cold hand in both of his warm ones.

"Ms. Evans!" he said. "I'm so glad you've returned. Please have a seat. I hope all is as well as it can be with your Maggie."

"She's hanging in there," she said. "My father's staying with her."

"Wonderful," he said. "That will be good for both of them. I'd be glad to help you in any way I can."

Virginia leaned forward in her seat. The counselor folded his hands on his desk and did the same.

"First I need to ask you a very personal question," she said. "Are you using a clone body, Mr. Indurane?"

"I am," he said, nodding slowly. "I hope this doesn't cause you any distress."

"Well, no," she said. "You're the first I've met, but my sister-in-law is going on a five-year research exchange to one of the nearest colonies later this week. We're thrilled for her."

"I would love to know more, perhaps even her name,

when the time is right," Mr. Indurane said. "She will be fortunate enough to see us in our natural form, and to see how we prepare for journeys from the most distant worlds to Earth and so many other planets. I've been here for three years of a seven year stay. I hope her experience will be as good as mine has been. To be honest, I'll be sad when my time comes to leave."

"Now I understand why you know so much about cloning," Virginia said. "And why you mentioned it for Maggie."

"There are new ways available now, similar to what we do to travel so far and stay so long." He pulled a folder down from the shelf to his right. "This leaves so much of the personality intact that people have been more satisfied with the results."

Virginia glanced at the photographs and text on the desk in front of her.

"But Maggie probably won't last long enough for cloning," she said. "I don't like the idea of cold storage. I know it works for space travel, but I don't want that for her."

"Time is of the essence here, yes," he said. "We've had great success with this technique over the last year."

Virginia shook her head. The thought of her girl in some kind of deep freeze hurt almost as much as her being gone forever. What if some part of Maggie knew she was trapped, but couldn't understand why she was cold and alone?

"There is another option, Ms. Evans," he said. "One that has only been tried a small number of times with your planet's life forms. What we need to produce is much smaller, and therefore faster."

"What is it, another kind of dog?" Virginia said, her heart sinking. "I wouldn't want to use one from a shelter or something."

"No, of course not," he said. "Thankfully almost all of

the shelters are empty. This is a different kind of host altogether."

He closed the file and folded his hands on top of it, looking into Virginia's eyes.

"The host would be you," he said.

Virginia blinked. "I don't think I understand."

"It's similar to our means of travel, of surpassing the weakness of a body not evolved for life on Earth. We're working with your scientists to develop the same technique for humans one day. For travel as far as Braxia, we must create a small seed. The holder of our consciousness. That crucial part allows us to continue on in the new body."

"Maggie would be conscious inside of me?" Virginia scowled before she could stop herself. "Wouldn't she be afraid?"

"It doesn't quite work like that with your pets," he said. "The awareness is much more diffuse, more general. The people who have pioneered this technique report an improved sense of well-being, of peace. The love they shared with their pet seems to continue to exist, but it comes from the inside."

Virginia looked at the photos lining the walls, at all the warm, innocent eyes. What had she said, that very morning? She wanted to put Maggie inside her heart and keep her forever. If any of this were true, this cloned traveler from farther away than she could imagine was offering her a chance to do just that.

"Does it always work?"

"We've had complete success so far," he said. "Partly because we're so careful with our screening process. You caught my attention because you grew up with Maggie. That bond is not easy to strain or break. But still you're compassionate enough that you're willing to let her go."

"What would happen to me, though?" Virginia said.

She fought the urge to rub her arms, wondering where this seed could possibly go.

"Your incision will be only be a few millimeters long and deep," he said. "We would need to draw a small bit of your blood to help the tissues match your body. We have Maggie's from this morning. The chest muscles provide a good location for feeding and sustaining the seed, as well as a lovely integration with the cultural beliefs of humans. My own is just here."

He covered the left side of his chest with his right hand. Over his nearly human heart.

"If you're asking me about your personality changing after the procedure, Virginia, we've seen no evidence of that, aside from increased confidence and security. One area we hope to investigate more over time is helping people who've suffered some kind of trauma. The bonds humans form with their pets are extraordinary, like nothing we've ever seen in our travels. Bringing such unconditional love into damaged minds may save sanity and lives."

Virginia's head was spinning, but her heart felt the hope she'd been missing since Maggie started slowing down a few weeks ago.

"Can we wait until my wife gets back?" she said. "This seems like a huge step to even think about without her here."

"That is where we'll run into a problem, Ms. Evans. In this case, cold storage doesn't work. The animal, much like us when we plan to travel, must be alive. Sedation is fine, but the consciousness must be in the body."

"I need a little time to think about this," she said. "What does it take to get started? I hate to bring money into something like this, but I saw what the vet school has to charge."

"We have everything we need except your blood sample and permission," he said. "There would be no cost. You and Maggie would be providing hope for peace and comfort to hurting people who have none. We would all be in your debt." He pulled out one more folder and handed it to her. "Contact information for those who've had the procedure. They have all volunteered to answer questions. My number is there as well. Please call me, any time of the day or night."

"Thank you, Mr. Indurane," Virginia said, getting to her feet. "I'm sorry, I need to think about this. Can you go ahead and start making this seed, just in case?"

Chapter 6

Virginia sat at home, Maggie's head in her lap, watching her breathe. Every single person on Mr. Indurane's list had been happy to talk to her. They'd all been remarkably happy in general, more than she'd ever encountered in a group of people who were all sober.

Not one of them reported any problems, and the handful of spouses who'd chimed in seemed pleased as well. The reasons not to do this amazing thing were dwindling with every rise and fall of Maggie's chest.

Wanting to talk to Gowri was the biggest obstacle left, one she couldn't resolve until several hours from now. Calling so far into the middle of the night would panic everyone for no good reason. If Virginia's memories of going out on the town with her in-laws were accurate, no one would possibly wake up enough to notice a text message.

She flipped the folder open and read over her scribbled notes. Everyone mentioned the security and confidence, the growing sense of being loved and appreciated. Maggie'd done that since she was a tiny puppy without even trying.

Virginia remembered being so shy and awkward as an early teenager, tentative to the point of being paralyzed in too many situations. Having something as simple as a dog to care for changed everything. Maggie had given more than Virginia could ever repay just by being herself.

Passing up this chance to at least try to return the favor felt harder by the minute.

"Come on, Mags. We both need to stretch and do our business." Virginia eased away and waited for her to get to her feet. "You ready, girlie?"

Maggie looked up without lifting her head and slowly wagged her tail. The deep brown of her eyes was surrounded by red. She made no move to get up.

"Wanna go outside?"

The dog thumped her tail again, then sighed and closed her eyes.

Virginia's chest felt hot and tight, far worse than at the vet's that morning, as if she were full of molten lead. Everything she'd read, heard from her vet, and what she knew in her heart told her this was her moment, whether Maggie made it for a few more hours, days, or even a week.

Dr. Martinez and Gowri had both said it. She'd be the one to know when Maggie's time was up. When she wasn't happy anymore.

Even if Maggie could be prodded off the couch and out the door, not wanting to do one of her favorite things in the world was the biggest sign so far. Her days had been long and joyful, and those days were coming to a close.

Virginia and Gowri had whispered together in the dark, making sure Maggie was asleep, both of them hoping their beloved pet would be lucky enough to pass away at home. Hoping she would close her eyes one night, safe and warm and loved, then slip away.

Virginia's only worry had been making sure her companion wasn't alone at the end. Now she was afraid of that happening before she could make up her mind. The only decision left was whether Maggie would live on in Virginia's memory or truly close to her heart.

Chapter 7

Virginia floated on a soft, warm cloud, her body seemingly a few inches above the reclined chair. Of all the countless times she'd visited the vet's office, this was the first time she was the patient.

"Will it hurt?" she said, trying to force her eyes open.

"You're already feeling the calming medication," Mr. Indurane said, "and you'll have local anesthesia, Ms. Evans. That will see you through with no discomfort. Most people are relaxed enough to fall asleep during the procedure."

"Call me Virginia, please. I mean will it hurt Maggie?"

The counselor's blue eyes swam into focus. She felt him move her hands onto Maggie's head resting on her tummy.

"She's right here, Virginia. She's asleep. My own consciousness has undergone this process many times. I experienced no pain or fear." He smiled. "Only joy upon awakening into a new world."

"I'm ready," she said, sinking further into peaceful darkness. "See you on the other side, Maggie girl."

Chapter 8

Virginia opened her eyes, not sure where she was. The lights overhead were dim, the room warm. She reached for Maggie as she'd done for half her life.

"She's gone, Virginia," Mr. Indurane said from beside her. "Is she still with us?"

Virginia blinked, trying to get past the soft fog in her brain. Of course Maggie wasn't gone. She was closer than she'd ever been before.

"She's right here," she whispered. "I feel her clear as day."

"Just so," he said. "We'll leave you here to recover a while longer. Everything went beautifully."

When he closed the door, she closed her eyes again, then carefully sat up. She didn't feel dizzy or sick, only confused. Virginia looked around the small room. There was nothing but the chair she was in, a space to walk, and cabinets.

"Where are you, Mags?"

Warmth flooded within her, mixed with excitement strong enough to make her heart beat faster. Virginia wasn't entirely sure why she was grinning. Maybe the medication that made her so woozy for some reason was still working.

She put her hand over her racing heart to feel a small lump high on her chest. A bandage peeked out from her shirt.

"Maggie?" Her jaw dropped as she gasped. "Oh my girlie, you are right here!"

Virginia finally remembered why Mr. Indurane said Maggie was gone. Tears threatened, but that innocent joy pushed them aside.

Such wonder, such acceptance. Such enthusiasm and gratitude for every breath she drew into her lungs. How could she possibly mourn the loss of a mere physical body when every single thing around her was so incredible?

Once she left this room, the world could only bring never-ending wonders. Virginia caught sight of red hair covering her jeans, the only thing Gowri had ever gently complained about when it came to their girl.

Oh, the pleasure of seeing her wife would surpass every-thing the great wide world had to offer.

Virginia Evans laughed hard and long enough to shed tears of joy for Maggie after all.

Terminalia

KARI · KILGORE

AUTHOR OF INTENTIONS AND LEGACY OF THE LAND

For my Atlanta family

Chapter 1

Kelly Webb lay in bed, eyes closed, wondering which pronoun would fit today. These few minutes first thing in the morning were the most comfortable of any day. Everything was undefined, so everything felt right. Stubble against the pillow answered the question.

He got up instead of hitting the snooze button again. Shaving always made the morning a bit longer. Kelly didn't understand what went on during the night or why, but going to sleep with facial hair of any length resulted in horrible acne as a woman. Knocking it back first thing made the bedtime rituals a little easer. He'd stopped worrying about his armpits and legs a long time ago.

He watched the dark red hair, much darker than on the rest of his body no matter what gender started the day, swirling down the drain.

Kelly grabbed his plain black phone off of a cardboard box beside the bed, leaving hers, the same model in a dark red case. Paying for two phones was a nuisance, but trying to deal with two lives on one phone was a nightmare.

He'd moved into the 1920s Craftsman bungalow in

Atlanta just a couple of months ago. The sturdy woodframe house had been restored without losing its graceful charm, but it was past time Kelly unpacked and made it a home. The place was still a cluttered jumble of half-emptied containers.

Having guests over would be tricky depending on what day it was, but he hated for a mess to keep him living like a hermit.

The phone's shared calendar was empty for both freelance gigs today. Finding a full-time job that would let him telecommute most of the time was proving harder than expected. Waking up as Mr. Kelly on a day when Ms. Kelly had to be at a mandatory meeting would redefine awkward.

Trying to keep a social life going was hard enough.

He realized he'd forgotten his slippers when his toes hit the rough, cold tile in the kitchen. That was one of the many strange little differences: he couldn't remember ever going barefoot as a woman. His feet got colder along with everything else.

The long grocery list on the refrigerator warned Kelly just before he opened the door. If he planned to eat, he was going out. He started the creaky old drip coffee machine and went back to get dressed.

The one thing he always arranged as soon as he moved in was the closet. He did his best to buy unisex clothing in similar neutral colors, but digging through trying to tell one pair of green khakis from another was a pain. Kelly wished for probably the millionth time that men's and women's clothes weren't sized so differently. His physical size didn't change all that much, with a few obvious exceptions, but he had to remember two numbers for everything.

He grabbed his brown wallet, leaving her black one on the counter, and headed out.

Chapter 2

KELLY KNEW he'd made a mistake as soon as the glass doors slid open. He usually went to a grocery story a few miles away as a guy, but he thought it was safe hours earlier than he was usually out.

Marlene, one of the women working behind the registers, smiled and started to wave, then looked confused and ran her hand through her wavy black hair instead.

Ms. Kelly had chatted quite a bit with Marlene, joining her on her breaks a few times, to the point that a date was the logical next step. If she'd recognized him, that was all over.

Damn. He should have skipped shaving at least.

Something about Marlene felt safe from the beginning, a connection Kelly rarely felt with anyone. She was cute, too, a few inches shorter than Kelly with a perfect curvy body and rich, dark skin.

Leaving now that she'd recognized him would probably just draw more attention to himself. He nodded, grabbed a cart, and walked around the corner to the produce section as fast as he could.

The other problem was this store was small compared to most of the vast food emporiums around the city. He kept glancing up to see Marlene watching him, dropping her gaze as soon as she noticed his attention. Kelly wished his hair changed as much as some of the more vital parts. With the short cut, he looked too much like his own twin.

Everyone who knew his female self in Atlanta would be surprised if he suddenly started wearing wigs for the first time in a few years, so it was too late for that. He never could stand the hot, itchy things anyway.

He stood just out of sight in the frozen food aisle, debating what to do. If he went to Marlene's register, even with no alcohol, she could ask for his ID before running his credit card if she was really curious. Once in a great while Kelly wished he'd used different names for his two selves despite the risk of mixing them up. If he avoided her on purpose, that might seem strange too. He took a deep breath and walked to the register beside hers.

Kelly thought he was going to make a clean getaway, but he felt a hand on his arm just as he got his receipt.

"This is going to sound so strange, and I'm sorry to bug you, but do you have a sister?" Marlene said, her warm green eyes making his knees a little weak.

Those kinds of reactions were definitely stronger on days like this, one of the reasons he'd always avoided being this close to someone who turned him on as a man and as a woman.

"I, uh, no. Just me."

"Wow, you remind me so much of someone I know," she said, her smile jumbling his brain a little more. "Any other family in town?"

"No, none at all. I just moved here. I don't really know any people. I mean, people here."

Unfortunately no one was in line at either register to stop

him from saying anything else silly. Marlene tilted her head to the side, and Kelly felt naked. Not in the good way he'd daydreamed about, but exposed in front of the world.

She nodded once, then reached into the back pocket of her jeans and handed him a business card.

"I think you're in exactly the right place. Most of us move down here for a reason." She started to turn around, then glanced back over her shoulder. "Hope to see you again soon."

Chapter 3

Kelly closed his front door and thumped the back of his head against the heavy wood. He muttered as he walked through to the kitchen, timing his steps to the words.

"You know better than this. What were you thinking? You *weren't* thinking—with your stomach, maybe, then with your crotch. No different than yesterday. Different shape, same stupid thoughts."

He put the groceries away, trying to slow his runaway brain. Beating himself up never helped anything.

He'd been trying so hard to do things differently here so he could stay for a while, arranging everything from the work he did to where he lived to how he shopped to avoid a mess just like this. Having to leave two colleges and three smaller cities after being careless apparently wasn't lesson enough.

"Relax, man! You're working yourself up over nothing. She just gave you a damn business card."

He sat down at the black granite island and pulled the card out, trying to get that nasty voice in his head focused on something else. It was white with black lettering, nothing special except the person who'd given it to him.

Debbie Kim, Relocation Consultant. We'll help you feel right at home.

Kelly tried to keep it under control, but hope that she'd given him the card *because* she recognized him churned in his belly. Maybe she'd recognized him, suspected who he really was, and wanted to know more instead of less.

Maybe.

The address was in the same neighborhood, about ten minutes away. Kelly stared out the window at the massive hickory tree in the back yard.

The thing was he did feel at home here, not only in the house but in the city itself. If ever a place were to accept him, her, however he woke up each day, he knew it would be Atlanta.

Something about the whole city seemed like a safe haven.

Well, maybe this relocation consultant would be able to help. He got out his phone. Marlene's smile in his mind gave him the courage to dial.

"Debbie Kim here. How can we help you?"

"Hi, um, Marlene, I mean, a friend of mine gave me your card?" Kelly grimaced, wondering when his powers of speech would recover.

"Wonderful. Satisfied clients are the best advertising anyone could hope for. I have an hour available at six this evening if you're ready to get started."

"Ready to… I'm not even sure what you do, Ms. Kim."

"That all depends on you. I will tell you Marlene's been a fantastic source of referrals for a few years now. She's never steered me or a new client wrong when it comes to the connections we all need in our lives."

Kelly glanced at the antique cat clock on the wall, the tail counting out minutes and hours longer than he'd been alive.

He had plenty of time today. And he was on the edge of

botching yet another fresh start for himself, one he wanted very much to make work.

"See you at six."

Chapter 4

AT TEN OF SIX, Kelly stepped out of sweltering late afternoon heat and seething rush hour traffic into another world.

The office was in a small house only a block away from the Centers for Disease Control. Instead of the typical diplomas on the wall, books jammed onto shelves, appropriate artwork sort of small office, this seemed like a home. An unusually neat and modern home, perhaps, with primary colors, steel, and glass everywhere, but still residential.

He was about to step back out to check the address when he heard sharp heels on the hardwood floor. The woman who walked in was a few inches shorter than Kelly, with gleaming black hair, upturned eyes, and dark red, theatrical lipstick to go with a matching long sheath dress.

"You must be Kelly," she said, holding out her hand, short nails painted dark blue. "I'm Debbie Kim."

"Kelly Webb."

"Come sit down, Kelly, and tell me about yourself."

He sat on a black leather chair with a low back and stammered out his usual story. Not much to tell: grew up in the Midwest, worked on computers, kept to himself. The only variation for the past several years had been the pronouns depending on how he woke up.

Debbie watched him the same inquisitive way Marlene had that morning.

He felt just as exposed.

"That's a lovely bit of fiction, Kelly, one of the best I've heard for a while," she said, but her voice didn't sound threatening. She held up one long-fingered hand when he opened his mouth. "No, it's quite all right. We all do what we have to until we learn we don't have to anymore. I did the same until I came here. Now, tell me why you chose Atlanta?"

"I heard good things about the city, I guess," Kelly said, trying to focus on what she'd asked instead of his life story being *fiction*. "Friendly people, lots of jobs, just about anything you need night or day. It seemed like a good place for a new start."

"Fair enough," Debbie said, inclining her head. "Many people find a home here they've never had anywhere else. There are reasons beyond counting for that, but I'm not going to waste our time trying to convince you. Some things are better seen and experienced."

"I'm sorry, but I'm still not sure what you do, or why Marlene sent me here." Kelly was fighting his reflexive fear of being discovered, and not very successfully. "What would you need to convince me of?"

"I mentioned earlier that Marlene is a wonderful source of referrals for me. Marlene is also a Spotter. She has a gift for recognizing people who've landed in the right place but need a little guidance to understand why. This will seem a bit forward, but did someone like a therapist or a doctor suggest moving here?"

The steel arms and back of the chair seemed like a slowly closing trap, and Kelly was fighting the urge to get up and walk out.

The most terrifying and desperate times in his life, when he was eighteen and struggling to understand what was happening to him in the middle of the night, weren't days he wanted to remember, much less answer questions about.

Knowing those awful conversations had saved his life didn't help.

"I heard it from more than one person, yeah," he said, managing to keep his voice level. "I paid to talk to a couple of them."

"They were trying to do the same thing I am, the same as Marlene. Every person, every living, thinking creature, contains a unique world, Kelly. We only bring strength and stability to each other by supporting the glorious, many worlds all around us. That's what draws those like us to a city like this. There's joy in our differences."

Kelly stared at her, trying to make sense of this surreal conversation. He needed to get away, to think this through.

The hints were as thrilling as Marlene handing him that card, but the prospect of being wrong was just as terrifying.

He'd wondered more than once why those therapists hadn't turned him in, locked him up, called in experts to perform medical experiments on such a freak of nature. He'd been too scared to ask why, not even of the ones who'd seen both sides of him.

"I need… I don't understand what's happening here," he said, getting to his feet.

Debbie didn't move.

"What you're feeling is perfectly normal. I won't tell you not to be frightened. I certainly was in the beginning. Before you go, let me ask you one last question." Kelly stopped at the door but he didn't turn. "Is there something you've tried to keep hidden? Something you've been afraid of another person knowing about since the day you figured it out for yourself?"

Kelly gripped the doorknob, gritting his teeth, cold sweat covering his body.

This could be a chance.

This could be a trap.

He didn't know enough to figure that out, but he needed to get out of here.

"Yes," he whispered, squeezing his eyes closed.

"Then I hope you'll listen to one more thing." He heard the leather sofa creak as Debbie get to her feet, but she didn't move toward him. "If you want to learn more, return to Marlene. You have a bond with her deeper than you know. She can show you the way."

"I'll think about it," he said in a stronger voice. "I will."

"Then turn around. Face me, Kelly Webb."

Kelly turned and gasped, falling back against the door. A much taller, slender, woman with nearly translucent pale skin and long, violet hair stood where Debbie had been mere seconds before. Her lipstick was the dark blue of her fingernails, and her eyes were glowing with the same shade.

This had to be the same woman, though. No one could have moved so quickly, certainly not in those noisy heels.

"Do you see me?" she said in Debbie's voice.

"I see you." Kelly swallowed, trying to catch his breath. "What *are* you?"

"I'm as human as you are, Kelly. I'm merely the sort of human I was born to be. Will you go to Marlene?"

Despite his earlier fears, he knew Marlene was his only chance to keep his mind in any kind of working order.

"I will."

"Then I'll see you in Terminalia."

She held out the card. Kelly stepped forward and took it, unable to look away from those luminous eyes. He backed out the door and closed it with a trembling hand, realizing he hadn't asked what on earth Terminalia was.

He breathed in the slightly cooler night air. He wasn't afraid, not really. What he'd just seen wasn't any stranger than his own life.

But his brain had definitely ceased operations for the rest of the day.

Kelly went home, drank a little more than he usually did, and went to bed.

He didn't forget to shave, though.

Chapter 5

Kelly didn't hesitate to check the state of things the next morning. No stubble, breasts instead of chest hair. She sighed, glad to be in the body of the first eighteen years of her life. Even though it was Saturday, she had no desire to sleep in.

Jumbled and anxious dreams of Debbie, Marlene, and her own body changing genders in the middle of the day in a gaping crowd of people had been quite enough.

She stared into the mirror for a long time, cataloging the differences in her features for the first time in years. Softer jawline, fuller lips, lighter eyebrows, and of course, no reason to get out the razor. Same big hazel-green eyes, just like her father's.

Could Debbie make changes like this, or was she always a woman? How the hell had she managed to transform herself at will to begin with?

Kelly had never found any reason or pattern for when she changed and no way to control it. One of her deepest fears was losing the strange reassurance of only sleeping overnight triggering the shift, maybe when she got older.

"Not sure what herbs and hormones to take for that," she said to her reflection, then laughed under her breath.

Kelly decided to put on at least a little makeup even before she admitted what she was going to do. Talking to Marlene wasn't optional—it was mandatory. If Marlene wasn't at work, Kelly would have to find her.

Did Marlene have the same kind of secret Kelly and apparently Debbie did? Hope twisted with fear in her gut, making her unease worse.

She purposely chose exactly the same outfit as yesterday, dark brown pants and blue t-shirt. For the first time in her life, at least since the first time she'd woken up terrified in a young man's body, Kelly *wanted* to be recognized.

Instead of walking right in like she did yesterday, Kelly stood outside the store in the bright morning sunlight, hoping to catch a glimpse of Marlene before running into her.

Debbie Kim's transformation was more than enough reason to go through with this, especially with her hints that she and Kelly weren't the only ones.

Her heart still pounded beneath her breasts, and she kept wiping her sweaty palms on her pants.

There! Marlene walked from the back of the store toward the registers, hair pulled back into a thick braid and dressed in street clothes.

Kelly closed her eyes and held her breath until her heart slowed down a little. She had no idea what she was stepping into, but she'd come too far to turn back. The freezing cold air inside the store helped settle her nerves a little more.

"Marlene? Sorry to bother you…"

Marlene turned, and her wide smile sent Kelly's stomach exploding into motion.

"You're far from bothering me, Kelly. I'm so glad you're here."

"I met Debbie yesterday."

"I heard a little bit about that," Marlene said, laughing and taking Kelly's hand. "She enjoys her dramatic moments."

"Dramatic is a good word for her." Kelly squeezed Marlene's hand. "I'm not going to get you in trouble with your boss, am I?"

"I'm not on shift for another hour. And I'll tell you a secret." Marlene turned her head from one side to the other, eyes wide, then winked. "My boss knows why I'm really here, and it's not to ring up overpriced organic produce." She started toward the door, and Kelly couldn't imagine anything besides following.

They walked around the corner to the employee break area, just a few picnic tables under a sprawling live oak tree. Kelly had been out here a few times already, taking every second she could to be with Marlene.

Her daydreams both as a woman and a man had been quite vivid and detailed, but she'd never dreamed up anything like this. They sat together at the table farthest from the parking lot, still holding hands.

"Do you want to ask questions or just listen to me ramble on?" Marlene said with a grin. "I've got a couple of things to ask you, too."

"Go ahead and ask," Kelly said before she could stop herself.

"When does it happen? Your change?"

Kelly opened her mouth, then smiled and tried again. "I haven't answered that question for a long time. Overnight, when I'm asleep. I never know until I wake up and, well, until I see what's there."

"Does it hurt?"

"It did at first. A lot." Kelly rubbed her jaw, remembering how her whole body ached for hours after a change for the first several months. "Kind of like growing pains, you know?

But it hardly ever does anymore. Can I ask you a question now?"

"Absolutely."

"Debbie said you're a Spotter. Do you change, too?"

Marlene watched a man with two small kids walk across the parking lot, then turned back to Kelly.

"No, nothing like that. My senses work differently. I think it's happened my whole life, but I didn't realize it wasn't normal until I was in high school. I don't just see people. I hear them—like a cello string vibrating. That's what makes me a Spotter, or did once I moved here and met Debbie. Tones for people like you and Debbie, and probably for someone else like me, are different. Typical people are more like a keyboard sound, smoother, digital. I heard you the second you walked in the first time."

"What did I sound like?"

Marlene smiled and leaned closer. Kelly forced herself not to move forward to kiss her.

"You have two tones, all the time, but I didn't know what that meant until yesterday. I heard you, but the lower sound was louder. Today the higher one is."

"Are there more of us?"

"So many more you can't imagine," Marlene said, nodding slowly. "Did Debbie tell you why a bunch of us are in Atlanta?"

"She mentioned a word, hang on a second. I can't remember it."

"Terminalia."

"Yeah, that's exactly what she said. It didn't make any sense to me, but that was the least of my worries once I got a good look at her. After she changed."

Marlene laughed, the musical sound stealing away a little bit more of Kelly's defenses.

"She has that effect on people, probably on purpose.

Atlanta was called Terminus a long time ago, but the word goes back a lot further. The name wasn't just about the railroads back then. Listen, are you busy tonight? Around nine?"

"Even if I was, I'd change my plans to be with you." Kelly was surprised by the words, but even more surprised it was the truth. She was glad her mouth was braver than the rest of her.

"Good, I'm glad to hear that," Marlene said, blushing a little. "Terminalia is sort of a party, a gathering every couple of weeks so new people can get to know the city and each other. Not everyone goes all the time, but most try to make it a few times a year."

Kelly remembered the last time she'd gone to a party, at least one that lasted past early evening. She was still attending college classes in person then, and she'd gone to bed with a woman as a woman.

Having to sneak out of a women's dorm early the next morning as a man ended her partying days.

After going to bed with a man then transforming into a man overnight nearly ended his life a few month later, Kelly was reluctant to date guys at all anymore.

"Everyone there is like us?" Kelly said.

"Either like us or involved with someone like us. Someone from CDC will be there tonight, that's a great way to learn more. She's a typical person, but she knows more than just about anyone else here."

"The CDC?" Kelly said, cold replacing the warmth in her belly, thinking of the huge glass and metal building not far from Debbie's house. "Is this a disease or something?"

Marlene laughed again, and this time she did kiss Kelly on the cheek.

"No, I'm sorry. That's, well, not really fake, but not the whole story either. I didn't mean the Centers for Disease Control. I meant Central Dimensional Coordination."

Kelly's jaw dropped, and Marlene squeezed her hand.

"I'm not handling this as well as I usually do," Marlene said. "I don't mean to dump so much on you, Kelly. It's just, I feel like I've known you forever. I keep forgetting you're new to all of this."

"I'm new to everything. Do you always feel that way? Like you've known people forever?"

"No, not like this," Marlene said, kissing Kelly's lips and stopping her whirling thoughts. "Nobody else sounds like you. Want to meet me here at 8:30 and we'll ride over together?"

Kelly nodded, her brain muddled and buzzing. She wished she could hear what Marlene sounded like right that second.

"I'd love to, Marlene."

Chapter 6

KELLY TRIED NOT to hold Marlene's hand too tightly as they walked into the party. Instead of a distant warehouse rave like she'd half feared, they were downtown in a soaring white museum. A young man at the door had a guest list, but he didn't even glance at it once he saw Marlene.

Kelly was glad she'd ignored the suggestion to dress casually. She'd changed into one of her few dresses at the last minute, dark purple and cut to flatter her woman's shape. Normal looking people around her wore everything from jeans to suits and ties, but Marlene wore a knockout little black dress.

Kelly was glad they both seemed to feel this was a date—huge party or not.

"You want to meet a few people or sit in on the talk?" Marlene said. "She doesn't take long, just enough to let us know how things are going." She dropped Kelly's hand long enough to grab two glasses of white wine.

"Let's go listen. I'm too nervous to talk to anyone else."

Kelly was afraid to drink the wine too fast, but she was delighted to have something to do with her free hand.

"You're going to be fine. You belong here, Kelly. Trust me. You'll like Dr. Standing. She can answer any questions you think up and a whole lot more."

By the time the two women found seats near the back, a middle-aged woman was pacing around the stage in the small auditorium, hands behind her back.

"Turning to our outreach programs, growing public acceptance and understanding of the multiverse is critical to our efforts to increase contact between the dimensions. I'm happy to report a breakthrough of sorts happened just yesterday."

She stopped in the middle of the stage, pushing strands of her gray hair back behind her ears.

"Dr. Evelyn Rowland, a prominent physicist and one of our strongest allies, was a guest on a national radio show. During her segment, she said the concept of a singular universe is so outdated that it should be retired from science."

Kelly was startled when everyone got to their feet and applauded. She'd been busy wishing she had a notebook so she'd remember what to ask and read more about later. She stood and joined in, smiling at Marlene's delighted whoop.

She whispered into Kelly's ear as everyone sat down, the warmth and brush of her lips sending chills through Kelly's whole body.

"Not very long ago, no scientist would have dared say something like that, even in private. You got here just in time for all the excitement."

"Yes, this is thrilling news," Dr. Standing said with a broad smile before she resumed her pacing. "Of course we all must continue discretion with the outside world, certainly outside of Atlanta, but having this idea in such a public forum shows how much progress we've made. Another sign is the number of new faces I see here and in the community in general. We'll be resuming orientation sessions next week to help our new arrivals get up to speed, and Dr. Rowland herself will be visiting in two weeks time for an in-depth review of what she and others have learned about the multiverse all around us."

She again stopped in the middle of the stage and looked slowly around the audience.

"I don't want to put anyone on the spot who still feels uncomfortable here, but I assure you you're among friends. If this is your first time attending, and if you'd like to, please stand."

Kelly froze, fear pinning her to the spot. She saw movement out of the corner of her eye. Almost half the audience was on their feet. Marlene caught Kelly's gaze and winked. Kelly took a deep breath and pushed up out of the seat.

After a few seconds, the rest of the crowd stood and applauded again, cheering a welcome Kelly felt throughout her strange and wonderful body. Several people around her reached out to shake her hand.

When everyone sat, Marlene put her arm around Kelly's shoulders. Dr. Standing wasn't the only one wiping tears from her eyes.

"The ancient Romans never could have imagined our modern world as they honored their Terminus, protector of boundaries. We come together here in our wonderful city of many worlds, someday a true city of the multiverse, to celebrate the differences that kept us hidden and alone for so many years. Our energetic field grows stronger every day, calling more souls to join us on all sides of the boundaries. Each and every one of you brings us closer to free contact between the dimensions. Thank you all, and welcome to this special celebration of Terminalia."

For the next several minutes, Kelly met more people than she had in the weeks since arriving in Atlanta. The last to approach was Debbie Kim—once again the small, dark-haired woman who'd first greeted her the evening before.

"I'm so glad to see you here," she said, pulling Kelly into an unexpected hug. "You're just as lovely as you were yesterday."

"Thank you for…giving me that little push," Kelly said, laughing, then turning to Marlene. "And thank you for showing me the way."

"I'll just leave the two of you alone then," Debbie said as she walked away, her knowing smile making Kelly blush. She didn't care who noticed.

"Are you okay?" Marlene said, her green eyes wide. "That was quite a big crowd for someone who seems so private."

"I think I'll sleep like a rock tonight, but I'm okay. What happens now?"

"That's it for the formalities, so everyone can relax and have fun. Let their hair down and be themselves, Debbie would say."

Marlene grinned as she took Kelly's hand and walked toward the open doors. The conversation and music noise level out there was rising.

"Ready to see what these people are really like?" Marlene said.

Kelly tried to get her head around the changes in the last couple of days, wondering if she'd ever be able to catch up.

She couldn't live as both parts of herself out in the open any more than she could have a week ago. But having even one person she could be honest with, and he could be honest with, was more than Kelly ever would have hoped for. A few hundred waited outside, with who knew how many more in the city surrounding them.

She'd have to think about the multiverse, the dimensions, once her mind settled down. And she knew she'd have a multitude of questions to ask Marlene, Debbie, Dr. Standing, anyone who'd listen and try to answer.

"I'm ready if you'll be with me," Kelly said.

Marlene stopped and pulled her into a kiss that took Kelly's breath. She drew back enough to look into Kelly's eyes.

"I'm hoping to be with you for a lot longer than one party."

"Even if I wake up as a guy tomorrow?" Kelly whispered, brushing Marlene's hair back into place. "I never know what's going to happen until it does."

"That's all any of us ever know, isn't it?" Marlene said with her irresistible deep laugh. "If I'm with you, none of that will matter. I'll be the luckiest girl in all the multiverse."

WICKED BONE
KARI KILGORE
AUTHOR OF SONGS IN THE MOUNTAIN & IN THE PINES

For Loretta

My very own Pashmina.

Chapter 1

THE BRIGHT WHITE ceramic tiles in the glorious, airy sunroom were one of Katie's favorite things about the vacation house high in the Virginia Blue Ridge Mountains. Light flooded in from three glass walls and the ceiling, making this one of the few places she felt truly warm so far north in the deep wintertime.

The angular, Art Deco lounge chairs and loveseat had matching white steel frames contrasted with deep, thick cushions in luscious, cheerful shades of every hue she loved. Blue, red, green, purple, and especially pink transformed the room from a beautiful if sterile white box into her little slice of personal heaven.

Even on painfully, unreasonably frigid days, the intense sunlight let Katie pursue her lifelong art and passion of gardening. Rich, earthy scents of jasmine and patchouli brought a welcome touch of her pride and joy, her sprawling prize-winning garden in Miami, to their frozen northern retreat.

The peppery bite of nasturtium lingered on her tongue. She couldn't resist munching on at least one of the gorgeous orange flowers every time she set foot in her Garden of Eden North. Thanks to Nora, their neighbor and caretaker while they were out of town, Katie's plants were always thriving.

Brilliant, marriage-saving compromises with her long-time husband Ken stretched far past her beloved white tile and rainbow of cushions in one spectacular room. Ken was out here as often as she was, enjoying the endless sea of mountains, blue and green and brown rolling and swelling as far as the eye could see in warmer weather.

Today crashing waves of brilliant white set off a soaring winter sky so blue it made Katie's eyes water. Well-planned and expensive construction paid off as the high altitude wind picked up. Glittering veils of ice diamonds danced across her view and over the transparent roof, bringing whispery sounds like sand skittering across the beach. Not the slightest trace of chilly air intruded no matter how hard that bitter wind tried to force its way in.

The house itself was a grand compromise, one Katie was thankful they'd come to the year she'd turned forty-five and Ken forty-three. She would have preferred a house further south than their home in Miami, maybe even the hedonistic, rum-soaked paradise of Key West. She still held out hope for that cozy, exclusive bungalow where the ghost of Hemmingway roamed free as the chickens.

Ken longed for the mountains of his childhood, though, and she had to admit he was right about the song and beauty of the rugged land. At the height of smothery, muggy summer in Florida, the cool breezes and chorus of frogs and insects up here were a symphony for her senses.

A soft, tickly caress across her bare feet, warmed by the fabulous radiant floor heating, reminded Katie of another much-loved compromise. She picked up a delicate, soft as cashmere, absolutely stunning solid black cat. Pashmina rumbled like she had a belly full of bumblebees, and she blinked her gorgeous deep green eyes slow as sweat rolling down a huge glass of summer afternoon iced tea.

Katie had never been a pet person until those emerald beauties claimed ownership of her heart as surely as Ken had.

"Glad to be back in the mountains, my Pashmina love?"

She held the dainty creature up to her ear, grinning as the purrs vibrated through her own skull. Pashmina batted at Katie's brown curls, then tried to pull her reading glasses from the top of her head.

"You're right, gorgeous girl. Mommy did come out here to do a little reading."

Katie headed toward her escapist and adventure corner, a huge purple beanbag piled high with rainbow pillows, and the delightful fantasy adventure novel she'd been dying to get back to. She loved anything but legal thrillers. Her real life job as an attorney made it far too clear that courtrooms were much more hurry up and wait than anything thrilling.

Before she took three steps, she froze.

There. Right there on her perfect, clean white tile.

Once in a great while, deep down inside her own mind, Katie remembered why she'd never wanted pets in the first place.

A smear of blood. A tiny fluff of grey fur.

A stomach no bigger than a dime.

Katie groaned. "*Why* can't you wait until Ken gets home?"

Pashmina blinked her seductive, languorous blink and purred even louder.

Katie put the vicious, murderous feline on the dark red loveseat. Appropriate match for such horrifying bloodlust.

"Good kitty," Katie said under her breath. Ken said she had to praise Pashmina for her excellent hunting feats, no matter how messy or how often. "Brave kitty. Clever girl."

Pashmina rolled onto her back, but Katie had finally

learned not to fall for that trap. Cat requests for a belly rub came with claws and sometimes teeth right behind.

The ways of the tiny house panther's hunts were still foreign and mysterious to Katie, and she thought they always would be. One day a delicate, pathetic foot lingered to announce the kill.

Another day, the tail. A head without a body. A body without a head.

In Florida Pashmina added lizards, huge insects, and an occasional scorpion to her menu, but continued her rejection of some random body part. Always proudly displayed where Katie would be sure to notice. No rhyme or reason to any of it.

Only bleach and gloves and scrubbing.

Chapter 2

Just as Katie stepped out into the gusting wind cutting through her indoor clothes like a hand through still water, she heard the jangling approach of Ken's Jeep. He'd bought a second-hand dark blue boxy monstrosity, outfitted with four wheel drive and pulleys and winches and everything else he could think up.

That was another idea of his that seemed strange to her at first, but it shifted into perfect sense and clarity after the first snowstorm up here.

The Jeep still looked horrid to Katie, and her ears recoiled from the irritating noise of the chains on the quiet winter day. And she was consistently amazed at how well that sturdy tank made it through the worst that winter or spring storms could throw at it. So far no creek was too flooded, no road too muddy, and no snow drift too high to stop Ken and his favorite mountain toy retrieved from his childhood.

She dropped the bag of distasteful guts and the paper towels she'd used to clean it into one of their three huge garbage cans. Ken was returning from hauling off the garbage among other things, so the small paper sack made a massive resounding thunk in the empty green canister. The frigid air damped down the musty, rotten smell that lingered no matter how clean the inside of the cans looked.

Katie flipped the raccoon guard - a bar that covered all three cans and kept their garbage inside rather than scattered all over the ground -down just as Ken's Jeep rounded the last curve of their steep graveled road.

He tapped the old-fashioned blaring horn once, and she heard the rough motor grind down into a lower gear. They left the grouchy old mountain goat here year-round, thank goodness, at her brother-in-law Dave's rustic cabin lower down the mountain. Her sensible and lovely grey Volvo waited in town for the return journey to warmer surroundings.

Katie couldn't imagine trying to make it to Georgia, much less all the way down the length of Florida, on those jouncy Jeep seats with plastic windows shrieking in her ears. She doubted the stubborn thing would make it to highway speeds even going down the miles-long mountain toward North Carolina.

"Hey there gorgeous!" Ken said as he pushed the Jeep's screechy door open. "What the hell are you doing out here in the cold?"

Katie realized her teeth were chattering, making her skull and her jaw ache.

"I heard you coming for the last three miles," she said, smiling without exposing her sensitive teeth to the awful cold. "I decided you deserved a hero's welcome for hauling the garbage away with your trusty battle-hardened steed there."

Ken leaned back in and grabbed two canvas grocery bags off the front seat. He wore a plaid-lined denim jacket and a goofy red wool cap with the ear flaps pulled down, both hand-me-downs from his grandfather. Katie couldn't see his red hair shot through with silver under the hat, but his mountain man beard only had a little bit of color left in it. She knew he'd shave every trace of it before they drove south, no matter how many times she said he looked more rugged and manly with whiskers, gray or not.

"I return to you in triumph, my Lady," he said, leaning down with a cold, bristly kiss. "Having dispatched the foul midden pit and secured wondrous feasts for our fair household."

"Bring them inside posthaste before they freeze solid, my Lord." Katie checked for a lurking Pashmina before she opened the glass kitchen door. Despite her pampered indoor life and variety of hunting conquests, the cat still sometimes tried to dart outside whenever they were here. "I'll start a fire to thaw all of us out."

"Seriously, why were you out there?" Ken said, hanging his coat and hat on the row of hooks by the door. His hair crackled with static. "It's just above zero."

Katie grimaced before she could help herself.

"Pashmina secured her own wondrous feast. She left me the most choice morsels, as usual."

Ken wrinkled his nose and caught her up in a proper, surprisingly warm hug.

"What bit did she leave this time? In the sunroom again?"

"Of course in the sunroom," Katie said, breathing in the wool and sweat and firewood scent of her husband. "She can't resist blood on white tile. The stomach most foul displeased Her Majesty today."

"I wish you'd leave that for me." Ken kissed her cheek and turned to help her put the groceries away.

Katie shuddered. "I can't stand to leave it all over the floor. I just wish I knew why she does this. The different bits, I mean."

"Because she loves you?" Ken winked as he opened the black refrigerator. "My brother actually reminded me today of what our grandmother used to say about things like this. Granny said every creature on God's Earth was born with a wicked bone."

"Every creature?" Katie stowed a bag of small red potatoes in their bin and turned back to him. "That sounds a bit extreme."

"Well, she did make an exception for whatever dogs she had at the time. Especially the redbone hounds. They were exempt. But every other critter had a wicked bone. Could be muscles or guts or whatever, and cats wouldn't eat that part. She said if they ate the wicked parts, they'd get too evil and mean to live around people."

"Not a cat person, huh?"

"My Granny? Not even a little bit. But she always had one to deal with the mice no one can keep control of out here. They were always black, too, just like your killer princess there. Maybe Pashmina knows how heartbroken you'd be if she turned all nasty on you."

Katie glanced toward the sunroom, and dark green eyes were indeed watching her. Pashmina sat in the doorway with her bushy, luxurious tail curled around her feet, giving every appearance of listening in.

"She's right about that," Katie said. She made the kissy noises her house panther loved, and Pashmina wrapped like liquid velvet around her ankles. "I wonder if it offends her when I throw them out."

Ken laughed. "Well, you won't be surprised to hear my Granny held firm beliefs on the matter. She said you had to get rid of whatever a cat left you, and right quick. That's one reason she hated it when folks around here started embalming humans instead of burying them right away. Remember how fast her funeral was?"

"I couldn't possibly forget. I had to cancel with an incredibly unsympathetic judge to make it up here in time."

"I appreciate that still." Ken kissed the tip of her nose. "Granny flat-out refused, made sure it was in her will that she would not be embalmed. She insisted on going in the ground quick even though she despised graveyards, so she could turn to dust straightaway. She was always onto us to never hang around or play in them, especially the big modern ones. All those wicked bones gathered up and preserved forever."

"So humans have wicked bones, too?"

Ken grunted. "Usually a lot more than one bone. You know that better than anyone, Madame Prosecutor. Wicked humans all over Florida are a big part of what paid for this little chalet."

Chapter 3

More than a decade of charmed winter travel luck disappeared when Katie and Ken, and Pashmina, returned for the holidays a month later. Even the valiant and much-maligned Jeep didn't stand a chance against several huge oak trees down across the road after a windy blizzard.

The original family homestead cabin could not have been a sharper contrast from the high-tech modern chalet. The few windows were low and small, but upgraded insulation and smooth, sheetrock walls let only a few drafts roar through. Once Katie bundled up in a scarf, sweater, and thick socks, she couldn't deny the charm of their temporary location while they waited for an overburdened road crew to arrive.

Her brother-in-law Dave kept fires roaring in a wood stove on each floor, and the spiced wine on top of the soapstone model downstairs provided a delightful welcoming smell and delicious warm treat. Katie and Pashmina set up housekeeping on the overstuffed sectional sofa near the fire downstairs, while Ken and Dave competed to see who could bring in the biggest armload of firewood.

With a stack of novels at the ready and a warm, rumbly

cat on her lap or curled up close to the wood stove, Katie had to admit this might be a tradition well worth repeating on future visits.

That cozy sense of family togetherness lasted until she realized just how many more mice could sneak in through the walls of the hundred-thirty-year-old cabin, modernized or not. And how much Pashmina enjoyed sharpening her claws and her hunting skills upon them.

The first catch seemed innocent enough. On the first night, with Ken and Dave both on their phones trying to track down anyone who could clear the massive trees, Pashmina dashed across the floor in front of Katie. She crouched in front of the fire, then batted a rounded shape from the thick blue hearth rug onto the dark, scarred hardwood floor.

A shape that moved and sounded like a plastic milk lid, one of the feline princess's less distressing toys.

A shape that seemed oddly brown and furry. Surely that was a trick of low light and travel weary eyes.

Both men were still in the small, bright yellow kitchen, pacing and talking into their mobile phones. Neither of them were smiling, so Katie decided to investigate herself. As was often the case when it came to her precious and puzzling dainty black cat, Katie regretted her curiosity immediately.

Pashmina jumped into her lap at the usual kissy sounds, silky tail high and waving her backside in Katie's face.

"What have you found, you spoiled rotten creature?"

The cat turned and dropped her treasure onto the clean white pages of Katie's latest science fiction mystery.

A perfectly preserved, lifelike, mummified mouse.

If Dave had a fireplace instead of the stove, she would have thrown the whole thing, book and all, into the flames. Instead she groaned and put the book, the mouse, and the cat on the paisley cushion beside her.

"Everything okay in there?" Ken said from the kitchen door. He still held his phone to his ear.

"No, not really. This vicious creature found... I don't even want to say."

Dave walked through the other kitchen door at her words, muttering into his own handset. He was a nearly perfect duplicate of his older brother, only with silvery black hair instead of red and a year-round beard. His uniform of flannel shirts over t-shirts, blue jeans, and hiking boots were year-round, too.

"Great, thank you," Dave said into the phone. "They'll be at my place. Call me if anything changes. What's wrong, Katie?"

She stood and pointed at the horrible thing. Right in the middle of her brand new book.

Dave stepped closer, scowling, then he picked up the mouse. In his bare hands.

"Wow, this must have been behind the stove," he said, holding it by the stiffened tail. "I haven't seen one like this in years."

"Nora says the power is still on, her place and ours," Ken said, standing beside Katie. "She'll check again tomorrow. Hey, a mouse mummy. I remember these from when Granny still lived here. Did Pashmina find it?"

"Yes, that cat found it," Katie said. She sat and held up her book to the bright lamp hanging over her shoulder and blew to get rid of any lingering fur. "She was batting it around like a toy."

Ken sat next to her, and to his credit, he was only smiling a little.

"Look at it this way, Sweetheart." He kissed her cheek. "Maybe she won't bring you the usual bits and pieces if she has this. You know, the fresh ones."

Dave put the mouse on the hardwood and pushed with

his fingertips. Pashmina pounced before it went more than a few inches. She trotted into the kitchen with the bizarre prize in her mouth, long black hair flouncing with her steps, growling the whole way.

"I'll pay you to keep us in mouse mummies if this works," Katie said.

A tiny gray tail curled up in her slipper in the middle of the night, not the least bit mummified, showed Katie how long Pashmina could hold up her end of the macabre bargain.

Chapter 4

THE NEXT DAY started off cold, clear, and with fresh wicked bone remainders in different parts of the cabin, all proudly arranged for best visibility and effect. Katie didn't hesitate to let Ken and Dave handle the cleanup and the requisite enthusiastic praise for her murdering beast.

She'd heard how cats had an unerring sense of who didn't want their attention at the moment, and Pashmina did spend every second as close to Katie as she could get. Or at least as close as Katie allowed with the eerily lifelike mouse mummy in constant attendance.

"Now you see why I have all the food in storage bins down here," Dave said, closing the front door. He dropped a huge armload of wood into the rack beside the stove, then leaned down to pet the source of so much slaughter. "Thank you, pretty girl. Maybe I need to get a couple of cats of my own to keep up her good work."

"Ken said your grandmother always kept a black one," Katie said. "Like this little murderer here."

"Oh yeah, this place was overrun with mice and snakes and everything else before I closed up the walls a bit. She let her cats outside sometimes, but they kept plenty busy in here."

"Snakes?" Katie said. "That's one of the few things she hasn't caught in Florida yet. I guess that means they can't get in the house, thank goodness. Do snakes have wicked bones?"

Dave laughed as he sat in his usual giant recliner close to the stove.

"A whole lot of folks say snakes are the original wicked bone, don't they?" Pashmina abandoned Katie and jumped onto his lap, mouse and all. "I figure snakes are working hard to eat up the mice, too."

"I never let this wretched demon outside," Katie said. "She does enough damage indoors."

"Granny didn't let 'em out often, afraid they'd catch the songbirds. She was strange about it, too." He scratched at his beard, staring into the fire. "I'd always hear her muttering to herself right before, but she never would tell me what was going on. I crept up behind her once, and I would have sworn I heard her say something like 'Get on out there and earn your keep. You best come back a cat.'"

A blast of cold air and low voices followed Ken into the house before Katie could ask what on earth that meant. A man Katie had never seen before was with him, smaller and more wiry than anyone in her husband's family. His face was clean-shaven, unusual in the winter in the mountains, but otherwise not all that remarkable.

"Katie, Dave, this is Jay Bishop," Ken said. He let Katie take the packages and bundles in his arms, results of a last-minute online holiday shopping binge. "He's on his way up to check on Nora's folks on the other side of the mountain. He should be able to clear our road tomorrow."

"Glad to do it," Jay said. "Gonna be up that way anyway, might as well take care of y'all while I'm at it. I can haul that wood back down here once the roads are all clear, stack it up for next winter."

His voice was soft and his accent was strange to Katie's ears, slower and more drawling than her in-laws. A cluster of three bright blue stones glittered from his right earlobe, same color as his eyes. Again, pierced ears on men wasn't unheard of even in the mountains these days. But the earring itself was striking enough to catch her attention.

"Happy to meet you, Jay," Dave said, reaching out to shake Jay's hand. "Even more happy you're in the tree clearing business. I'll sure take you up on the firewood. But I guess it should go up to their house since it's their road blocked."

"We'll split it with you," Ken said, clapping his brother on the back. "Least we can do for you putting up with us. Just let us know when it's cleared, Jay, and we'll settle up."

"I'll sure do that," Jay said. He nodded at all three of them right before he stepped out the door. "I thank you."

"How did you find him?" Dave said. All three of them filed into the kitchen to refill coffee and get lunch ready. "Everyone I called last night was booked solid."

"Yeah, me too," Ken said. "I heard him talking to someone else at the post office about heading up the mountain. I knew if I didn't find someone fast, we'd be stuck here for another week under your feet."

"You're good company, pretty much," Dave said. "Especially if it means firewood for next year. Pashmina's not quite finished clearing the place out for me yet."

Katie watched the silky animal pacing back and forth over the poor, petrified mouse. Pashmina growled every time she got close to the husked out creature. She finally stopped and hunched down in her familiar pounce mode, the front of her body low, wriggling rear high with her tail waving. The cat jumped toward her distressing toy, snatched it up, and ran into the bathroom.

That night, Pashmina finally disposed of her mouse mummy. Everything vanished except the feather-light head proudly displayed in the middle of the bathtub.

She also started the determined habit of sneaking outside that would shatter Katie's understanding of reality forever.

Chapter 5

No matter how carefully Katie, Ken, Dave, or anyone else checked before they opened the door, Pashmina managed to dart through and away. She didn't go far at first, at least not while the snow was still on the ground. By the time Katie and Ken got back to their house and muddy yard, the cat stayed out longer every time.

"She can't keep this up in Miami," Katie said when they were in bed on Christmas Eve. Pashmina was curled up on her belly, rumbling and content. "A gator will get her."

"Or a car. We may have to block her into certain rooms. I don't want to scare you, but there are plenty of critters here that could hurt a small cat like this."

"I know." Katie stroked the soft fur, crackling with static in the dry air. "Hawks and bobcats and stray dogs. Are there mountain lions still? Like the panthers in Florida?"

She felt Ken shaking his head.

"Not anymore. They got hunted out almost a hundred years ago. Nothing but rumors of people letting pet ones loose, but nothing ever comes of it. She's safe from that much up here."

Katie scratched under the cat's chin, smiling at how she tilted her head back and forth to exactly the right spot.

"Just like everything else," she said, "I wish I knew *why* she's doing this."

But Pashmina didn't even try to get out when they returned to Florida after New Year's Eve. She settled back into her usual routine of hunting what came into the house and only halfheartedly watching the door.

The frequency of bloody offerings returned to normal, too. Katie hadn't realized until then how much they'd dropped off with the house panther's forays into the outdoors.

Their spring getaway in the mountains, and renewed feline escapes, had her wishing for the typical cat trophies after the first night.

Katie walked into the bright sunroom, mind on an upcoming trial, eyes on the first pinkish blush in the hardwood trees all around them.

She nearly stepped on a shriveled and twisted index finger.

When a soft tickle caressed her ankle, Katie clapped her hand over her mouth to keep from screaming. No mistaking it, and no pretending it was some kind of animal remains. The flesh was wrinkled into grayish leather, the long fingernail coated in dirt.

Pashmina slinked toward the horrible relic. Katie grabbed her and held her against her chest.

"Where did you get that?" she whispered, frozen to the spot. "You can't possibly be digging up graves now."

She backed up, clutching at the purring cat and unable to look away from the thing on the white tile.

At least there was no blood.

Katie misdialed several times before she managed to dial Ken's mobile. Pashmina continued to purr, eyes closed. She kneaded Katie's shoulder, one foot, then the other, over and over.

"Hey sweetheart," Ken said on a miraculously clear connection. "What's up?"

"Can you come home now, please?" Katie said. Her voice trembled in time with her heartbeat. "If Dave's with you, bring him too."

"What's going on, Katie?" Ken sounded stern, his normal response to being scared to death.

"Just hurry, please. Pashmina found something I need your help with. Okay?"

"We'll be right there."

Katie sank onto one of the overstuffed orange chairs beside the window, still staring at the finger. The *human* finger that was somehow inside her house. She only looked away long enough to verify that her sweet, precious cat was sound asleep on the sofa before Ken and Dave stormed into the house barely ten minutes later.

"Katie, thank goodness." Ken knelt beside her. "What's wrong?"

"I think I know," Dave said. He stood over the thing, shaking his head. "When did this show up?"

"Sometime after Ken left," Katie said. "She got out again, so I left the sunroom door cracked like we have been. I don't know when she got back. Where the hell could she even find that?"

"Only thing I can think is one of the old family cemeteries," Dave said. He squatted and stared at the displaced remains. Katie was thankful he didn't pick it up like he had the mouse mummy. "They're scattered through the mountains up here. Doubt anyone knows about them all."

"But aren't the bodies supposed to be buried?" Katie said. "I'm quite sure she didn't dig that up by herself."

"Normally, yeah," Ken said. He squeezed Katie's shoulder, then stood beside his brother. "Something else must have got to this first."

"Should we call someone?" Katie said. "The police, or… I don't know who."

Dave rubbed at his beard, nodding.

"I'll call Sheriff Meade. Even if someone's digging a foundation or something, they need to know what they're actually into."

"Go ahead," Ken said. "I'll take care of this."

Katie wanted to go in the bedroom and lock the door, or maybe lock herself into the bathroom and take a scorching hot shower. But she was afraid if she didn't watch, she'd have nightmares about finding the finger all over the house.

In her shoes. Under her pillow. Inside a box of cereal.

She watched without saying a word while Ken used a pair of her blue kitchen gloves and dropped the shriveled thing into a plastic baggie. When he stepped outside to give the baggie to his brother, still pacing and talking on his phone, Katie got up to grab her bleach. Desiccated or not, she had no desire to wonder if she was stepping on what was left of someone's great-great something or other every time she walked into her sunroom.

When she came back from the kitchen, Pashmina stood on the white tile where she'd left her latest trophy. She'd never seemed to care when Katie got rid of the horrible evidence before. This time she sniffed all around the spot, chirping to herself. Pashmina sneezed, then trotted out of the sunroom.

"Let me do that, hon," Ken said, walking in with Dave right behind him.

"Thank you, but I'll feel better if I do. What did the sheriff say?"

Dave shrugged, shaking his head.

"She doesn't know of anyone digging for a foundation or

a well right now. Sometimes folks work without a permit, though. She's going to come up tomorrow and have a look if that's okay with you."

"Of course it's okay with me." Katie snorted, trying not to breathe in too much of the harsh bleach as she scrubbed. "Even if this slaughter queen wasn't bringing human body parts inside now, I don't like the idea of a bunch of open graves no one knows about."

"You know who we might want to ask," Ken said. "The kid who cleared our road over the winter. Brought us both a bunch of firewood?"

"Yeah, Jay Bishop." Dave had his phone out already, scrolling the screen with his thumb. "He has all the equipment you'd need, bulldozer and backhoe and everything. Seems like a good guy. I'm pretty sure he'd admit it if someone was paying him under the table to work without a permit. Or if he'd turned someone down for the job."

Katie sighed and gave the floor a last swipe, finally satisfied no possible trace of the grave remained.

"I'm sorry I interrupted whatever you boys were doing. I think I'll be okay up here with my dark archeologist if you want to get back to it."

Ken put his arm around her waist and kissed her cheek.

"You sure? We were just knocking around the old home place, clearing out Granny's old garden patch."

"I'll be fine," Katie said. "My head was deep in lawyer stuff when I almost stepped on Pashmina's latest treasure. You know I'm rotten company at times like that. If fresh veggies are in it for us, go, dig."

For the first time in days, Pashmina didn't linger by the door or try to dart out. Katie found her sound asleep on her cushion in front of the wood stove. The cat didn't twitch a whisker for the rest of the night.

Chapter 6

Sheriff Meade turned out to be the kind of law enforcement officer Katie most liked working with on criminal cases. Calm, steady, and unruffled by whatever strange thing might be going on around her. She was Katie's height, too, with gleaming blonde hair caught back in a thick braid down the back of her brown uniform.

She even took notes on her smart phone rather than the tiny flip notebook most officers still seemed to use. Katie liked her immediately.

"I'll ask around," the sheriff said as she, Katie, and Ken walked in a circle around the house. "Have folks up here keep an eye out for muddy tracks or anything else strange. It could be something as simple as a big tree dying during a bad winter. The ground stayed frozen solid until a couple of weeks ago. That makes it heave sometimes. Do you happen to know which direction she runs off to?"

"I have no idea," Katie said. "By the time I chase after her, she's out of sight."

"Well, the tree line's close to the house all around," the sheriff said. "Makes sense. If you do catch her going a certain way, be sure to let me know. Cats can be the devil to keep inside once they get a taste for sneaking by you. We'll see what we can figure out."

Pashmina darted out when Katie took the garbage out that evening, only returning sometime in the middle of the night. The mossy, earthy smell of her fur when she jumped up on the bed sent Katie stumbling through the house, searching for whatever fresh horror her happily purring cat had returned with. Nothing, fresh or dried.

The next morning, what looked like a clump of leathery leaves with long bits of grass attached waited in the middle of the sunroom.

When Katie poked it with the broom and it flopped over, she finally did scream.

What Pashmina brought home turned out to be a bit of scalp and hair.

The macabre offerings continued throughout the week, and Pashmina's determination to get out only grew stronger. Katie found another finger, two toes, and an ear, all wrinkled and dried out.

She and Ken talked to Dave about having an entryway built when they left to try to keep the mighty feline explorer under some kind of control. No one loved the idea of breaking the clean lines of the house that way, but a double set of doors, the closest they could get to a kitty airlock, might actually work.

Neither the sheriff or any of the landowners could track down where the lost bits were coming from, not even on surveyor's maps. Katie started to dread her sunroom and what offering would await.

Her imagination and bad dreams didn't prepare her for what Pashmina did leave next.

At first, she thought her pet had returned to her former

habit of mice. Katie never dreamed she'd be relieved to see a bloody smear on the tile. Her relief didn't last long.

The afternoon sun was dim with the sky heavy and overcast, threatening a late season snow. Katie was nearly upon the mess, scrubbing supplies in hand, before she turned on the light.

"Ken!"

She staggered back, and only the overstuffed chair behind her kept her from falling.

Pashmina jumped down from Katie's reading corner, purring and rubbing against the wall, the couch, everything she walked by.

Katie tried control herself, but she was nearly hyperventilating by the time her husband ran around the corner.

"Katie? What's wrong?"

She could only point with one hand. The other covered her mouth in a desperate attempt to keep her lunch where it belonged.

The bloody thing on the floor wasn't part of a mouse or a squirrel or even a bird.

A fresh human ear joined the long list of horrifying trophies.

"What the *hell?*" Ken fumbled and nearly dropped his phone. "Don't touch anything until Sheriff Meade gets here."

"Don't worry," Katie whispered. She gritted her teeth, but her delirious mind wondering whether the ear was still warm was too much. She barely made it to the bathroom.

By the time she rinsed her mouth out and washed her face, Ken was in the kitchen. He'd locked Pashmina in the bedroom. Katie hated to admit it to herself, but she was relieved.

The idea of the fastidious creature delicately cleaning blood off her fur almost got her stomach started again.

"The sheriff will be here in an hour," Ken said, running his fingers through his hair. "Dave sooner."

"I don't understand this. Sheriff Meade said no one's been buried up here for a long time, didn't she? That looked…" Katie paused for a deep breath. "That looked a lot fresher than even from a funeral home."

"Well yeah. They would have drained…never mind. Get some water or something, Sweetheart. You still look green."

Katie laughed, amazed at such a bizarre response under the circumstances.

"My dear, water simply will not do. I'm making myself a nice, cold gin and tonic. Want one?"

Ken stared at her for a second, then he smiled.

"I'll take you up on that as soon as Sheriff Meade leaves."

Dave showed up around the time Katie finished her drink, but before she could decide whether or not to have a second.

"I'm sure we had a bad connection there," he said, brushing snowflakes from his beard and shoulders. "You didn't say a *fresh* human ear, did you? Tell me you didn't."

"Afraid so," Ken said. "Go have a look for yourself."

Dave returned a few minutes later, shaking his head.

"I'll be damned. You said Sheriff Meade is on her way, too?"

"Should be here any minute," Ken said. "So what would Granny have to say about this one, Dave? You heard a lot more of her tales than I ever did."

Dave raised his thick black eyebrows, the corners of his mouth turning down.

"This one might be beyond even her wisdom. I don't think any of Granny's cats ever brought back anything quite like this. Or if they did, she didn't tell me."

"The wicked bone," Katie said under her breath.

"What was that?" Ken reached for her hand. "I couldn't hear you."

"Dave told me about your grandmother saying everything and everyone had a wicked bone. The parts the cats won't eat."

Ken nodded, but now he looked worried.

"Right," Dave said. "Everything except her dogs."

"Except her dogs," Katie echoed. Her head felt swimmy and her skin too hot, but not from the gin. "Maybe this is the part of whoever that was. The part the cat won't eat."

"I don't understand," Ken said. "You're not making sense, Katie."

"You think I don't know that?" Katie smiled to soften the words. "Come with me. I want to get a closer look at…it."

Ken started to argue, but she touched his lips with her fingertips.

"I'm serious, and I'm not drunk. Come on."

Both men followed her, and Katie was sure they glanced at each other behind her back. For once she didn't care. Something had hold of her mind, her Lawyer Mind she called it. She'd learned a long time ago to pay attention when that happened.

She didn't let go of Ken's hand, though.

"Do you have your phone?" she said, standing a few inches away from the blood. "Either of you?"

"You want pictures?" Dave said.

"Not pictures. The flashlight."

Dave shrugged, pulled out his phone, and thumbed the light on. Katie leaned as close as she dared, not wanting to breathe in the metallic scent. Curious as she was, that would set off her jumpy stomach again for sure.

"What is that?" Ken let go of her hand and squatted, both of his knees crackling like gunshots. "Something glinting."

"We shouldn't touch anything," Dave said, stepping forward himself. "Not until the sheriff gets here."

"I see it too," Katie said.

She leaned closer, her hand on Ken's shoulder.

There, on the red-streaked earlobe.

Three tiny blue stones.

Katie's head floated again, and she clutched at Ken to keep from staggering into the mess.

"Dave," she said, "did you ever ask that guy about the graveyards? The tractor guy?"

He looked confused for a second.

"You mean Jay Bishop? No, I didn't get a chance to. Not really. I left him a voice message last week. Haven't seen him or heard back."

"He had an earring like that." Katie pointed at the ear. "Just like it."

"You don't think…" Ken said.

"Which way did he live?" Katie said. "Which way from here? Do you know where his house was?"

The rolling queasiness in her belly gave way to a cold, solid certainty. Katie couldn't explain it, even to herself.

But she *knew*.

"He…hang on." Dave rubbed at the bridge of his nose, the same way Ken did when his was confused and trying to pull it together. "He said he'd moved into the old Blevins place, but that was months ago. West. It's to the west."

"Then let's go see," Katie said. "Before the snow gets too heavy."

The two men followed her only a few seconds behind, and she was thankful they didn't argue first. Her Lawyer Mind insisted she was still on the right track, while her regular mind and the rest of her insisted she was crazy.

They walked less than a hundred feet to the west through huge snowflakes floating in slow motion. The ground wasn't covered yet, but it would be before the sun went down.

At the edge of the woods, the grass gave way to leaves and brushy undergrowth.

And a massive, flattened spot in the brush, turning each flake scarlet as soon as they touched the ground.

"Katie, what…" Ken said, staring at the ground. "How did you know to look here?"

"I didn't. But Sheriff Meade said to see if we could catch which way Pashmina ran off."

"Pashmina didn't make anything that big," Dave said.

"Something did." Katie pointed to flattened spots leading away from the blood, heading onto the grass and toward the house. The snow was filling them in already, but the shape was unmistakable.

Giant paw prints.

Like a panther's.

"That's too big to be a bobcat," Dave said, his voice barely above a whisper. He started to kneel and ended up on his knees instead. He held his hand over one of the tracks, barely covering it. "Or any kind of dog."

"What did your Granny say when she sent her cats out?" Katie said. "Go out and earn your keep, and something else?"

Dave looked up at her, eyes wide and face pale.

"Come back a cat. She said best come back a cat."

Ken shook his head and crossed his arms.

"What, you're saying a panther did this? Something to do with Granny's tall tales?"

"I don't know," Katie said. "But where did the tracks go?"

All three of them stepped backward, staring down at the rapidly disappearing grass. The huge footprints were still visible heading right toward the house. Toward the sunroom door they'd been leaving open when Pashmina darted outside.

The tracks stopped about ten feet away from the woods.

"We have to tell Sheriff Meade," Ken said, still shaking his head. "None of this makes any sense."

"It doesn't make sense to me, either," Katie said. "But as your attorney, I'd advise you to think about how this looks first. A severed ear in our sunroom, and a big blood puddle right beside the house?"

"What are we supposed to do, then?" Ken snapped. "Pretend we didn't see any of this?"

"Hang on." Dave grabbed Ken's shoulder. "I'm not saying I think… I'm not saying *what* I think because I can't. But maybe the sheriff should check the place out. Where Jay was staying, I mean. She'd need to go there anyway, right?"

"How long til the snow covers this up?" Katie said. "The blood, the tracks?"

"Just a few minutes at this rate." Ken rubbed his eyes, then glanced at the blood again. It was already turning pink, well on its way to white. "I can't believe I'm even considering this."

Katie snorted, trying not to laugh out loud.

"After Pashmina has been bringing body parts into the house for days? What I'd consider has adjusted itself considerably. Let's get back inside. We won't even know what we're suggesting until someone finds this Jay person. Or gets a look at his house."

Chapter 7

The house was the key to everything.

Sheriff Meade showed up less than half an hour later in her official brown version of Ken's Jeep, with two deputies riding along. Katie tried not to let her relief show when one of them recognized the blue earring before she had to point it out. They headed right out to look for Jay Bishop.

By the time they returned, pale and quiet, the snow had wiped out all evidence of blood and huge paw prints beside Ken and Katie's house.

None of that mattered after what the officers found over at the old Blevins place.

Sheriff Meade and the two young men with her sat around Katie's kitchen, cooling mugs of coffee gripped in their hands.

"The door was open," the sheriff said. "There was blood there and out into the yard. Not a trace of anything else, though. No bodies."

"He'd seen plenty of bodies at some point," one of the deputies said, his voice trembling.

Sheriff Meade nodded.

"That Blevins place never was much more than a single-room cabin, but he had it stuffed full. Boxes full of old jewelry, gold teeth, wire-frame glasses. Still musty and stinking of the bodies they were buried with. None of it worth a lot by itself, though some of the diamonds and such would have added up. But enough to get your attention. Looked to me like he was packing up to leave. We would have heard if something like this happened at the big cemeteries in town."

"Something like what?" Ken said. He held his own mug, and Katie was sure she'd seen him pour a shot of whiskey in.

"I suspect he'd been digging up the old family graveyards," Sheriff Meade said. "That would explain the things your cat brought home, too. That little backhoe he had was light enough to make it up the trails, especially when the ground was frozen. I expect we'll find he wasn't as careful putting things back together when he was finished."

"A grave robber," Dave said. "In this day and age."

"Still don't know where the ear came from," the sheriff said. "Or where the rest of him went. But we'll keep looking."

"I hope he's gone for good," Katie said, getting to her feet. "Excuse me for a second?"

When she opened the bedroom door, Pashmina wasn't curled up on Katie's pillow sleeping, the way she usually did when she was alone. The silken black cat waited just inside the door, tail curled around her feet.

She blinked up at Katie, long and slow.

Ken always said they had to praise Pashmina for a successful hunt.

"What have you been doing, gorgeous?" Katie picked up the intelligent, wondrous creature. "Taking care of the problem yourself when the humans were too silly to catch all the hints you left for us?"

Pashmina only purred, settling herself onto Katie's shoulder.

She kneaded with one tiny foot, then the other, over and over again.

ABOUT KARI

Kari Kilgore's wanderlust and imagination lead her all over the world on grand adventures. Her heart and family bring her home to her native Appalachian Mountains of Virginia. From that solid base, she and her husband Jason A. Adams bring those adventures to life in fiction.

Kari writes science fiction, fantasy, horror, and contemporary fiction, and she's happiest when she surprises herself. She lives at the end of a long dirt road in the middle of the woods with Jason, various house critters, and wildlife they're better off not knowing more about.

The Confidential Adventure Club

For Kari's exclusive free After The End stories, deleted scenes (including one for *Terminalia*, one of the stories in this collection), discounts, early pre-sale releases, adorable pet photos, and a whole lot more not available anywhere else, visit The Confidential Adventure Club at www.smarturl.it/c-a-club-welcome.

Hope to see you there!

www.karikilgore.com
www.spiralpublishing.net

ALSO BY KARI KILGORE

I hope you enjoyed reading *Fantastic Shorts: Volume 1* as much as I enjoyed writing it. Check out more of my fiction at www.karikilgore.com.

The Confidential Adventure Club

Want more fiction from Kari, including stories, discounts, and box sets not available anywhere else? Want to hear about locations, research, and other cool things that inspired these stories and beyond? All that and adorable pet photos, too?

Join The Confidential Adventure Club and get a thank you gift of a free short story and a whole lot more at www.smarturl.it/c-a-club-welcome.

Hope to see you there!

Novels:

Until Death

The Dream Thief

Dreaming the Storm: Book One of the Storms of Future Past Series

Joining the Storm: Book Two of the Storms of Future Past Series

Fighting the Storm: Book Four of the Storms of Future Past Series

Novellas:

Songs in the Mountain

Legacy of the Land

Restricted Species

The Becalmed

In the Pines

Into the Storm: Book Three of the Storms of Future Past Series

Short Stories:

Renovations

Intentions

The Garbage Belt

The Seeds of Love

Wicked Bone

The Sound of Murder

Terminalia

Little Five: A Terminalia Story

Reflections

Collections:

Fantastic Women: A Dark Fantasy Novella Trio

> "Kari Kilgore is an author to watch—her lyrical voice a siren song; her insight, conjured voodoo."
>
> —Richard Thomas, author of *Breaker* and *Tribulations*

ADDITIONAL COPYRIGHT INFORMATION

Intentions

Copyright © 2018 by Kari A. Kilgore

All rights reserved

Published 2018 by Spiral Publishing, Ltd. www.spiralpublishing.net

Book and cover design copyright © 2018 by Spiral Publishing, Ltd.

Cover art copyright © 2018 by Migutas/Dreamstime.com

ISBN-13: 978-1721863471

Reflections

Copyright © 2019 by Kari A. Kilgore

All rights reserved

Published 2019 by Spiral Publishing, Ltd. www.spiralpublishing.net

Book and cover design copyright © 2019 by Spiral Publishing, Ltd.

Cover art copyright © 2019 by Andrey Kobylko/Depositphotos.com

ISBN-13: 978-1090527578

The Seeds of Love

Copyright © 2018 by Kari A. Kilgore

All rights reserved

Published 2018 by Spiral Publishing, Ltd. www.spiralpublishing.net

Book and cover design copyright © 2018 by Spiral Publishing, Ltd.

Cover art copyright © 2018 by WarmTail/DepositPhotos.com

ISBN-13: 978-1983263002

Terminala

Copyright © 2019 by Kari A. Kilgore

Published 2/23/2019 by Spiral Publishing, Ltd. www.spiralpublishing.net

Book and cover design copyright © 2019 by Spiral Publishing, Ltd.

Cover art copyright © 2019 by Domiciano Pablo Romero Franco/Dreamstime.com

ISBN-13: 978-1796912296

Wicked Bone

Published 2018 by Spiral Publishing, Ltd.

www.spiralpublishing.net

Book and cover design copyright © 2018 by Spiral Publishing, Ltd.

Cover art copyright © 2018 by Copyright Nikolas217 | Dreamstime.com

ISBN-13: 9781092510752

Library of Congress Control Number: 2018913209